T0275006

ENCLOSURE ARCHITECT

ENCLOSURE ARCHITECT

A NOVEL

DOUGLAS W. MILLIKEN

West Virginia University Press • Morgantown

ISBN 978-1-959000-21–1 (paperback)
978-1-959000-22-8 (ebook)

Library of Congress Cataloging-in-Publication Data
Names: Milliken, Douglas W., author.
Title: Enclosure architect : a novel / Douglas W. Milliken.
Description: Morgantown : West Virginia University Press, 2024.
Identifiers: LCCN 2024009326 | ISBN 9781959000211 (paperback)
| ISBN 9781959000228 (ebook)
Subjects: LCGFT: Novels.
Classification: LCC PS3613.I56285 E53 2024 | DDC 813/.6--dc23/eng/20240301
LC record available at https://lccn.loc.gov/2024009326

Portions of this novel previously appeared in an earlier form as
"Mechanism of Perfection" in *Bridge* 22, no. 1, 2022, and as
"Moonlighting" in *Matter Press*, 2019.

Cover design by Than Saffel / WVU Press based on a drawing by Douglas
W. Milliken. Page design by Than Saffel / WVU Press

For my friends and collaborators, those who remain
and those who remained behind.

CONTENTS

Center 1

Periphery 7

Plane 37

Insideness 65

Outsideness 83

Containment 159

Acknowledgments 229

ENCLOSURE ARCHITECT

CENTER

I'M WILLING to accept that this is—that I am—the result of environmental chemistry, that who I am right this second is determined, in an equal or greater proportion to the history of my choices and the memory of their choosing, by the clear winter sky conspiring with the tall windows of this vaulting space to create a thermal gain in such opposition to the outside air, light blading all around me— Oh hell, this isn't an undergrad's artist statement: Who can fight the low-grade yet pervasive ecstasy of vitamin D? The windows make the sun feel good to me, so for the immediate present-tense me, remembering feels good too. Like the first summer when we—all of us—set ourselves loose like freed zoo animals into the abandoned and abandoning parts of this city, giddy on the potential promised in the real-ass (albeit vague) revolution happening somewhere around us. When we could prowl the abounding vacancy and find, to our amazement and fortune, cases of beer still cold in the defunct coolers of blasted bodegas, backyard gardens riotous with fruit and bloom forgotten when the households fled for cover, pints of Old Granddad in deserted sock drawers no one had opened in weeks. When we could scavenge and luxuriate in our scavenging, TC and I in a dumpster behind an active juice factory or boutique grocery or uptown bakery, flashlighting in the dark to check for mold or expiration dates before tossing our cull to Denver and Hannah on the midnight pavement outside. When I could find all the clothes I liked by raiding the houses of long-evacuated Catholic families, constructing a wardrobe of pilfered First Communion suits while every other dork wore corduroys and sweaters over collared shirts. When I could tell when and to what degree a woman wanted me by the way she tugged and snapped my suspender straps. When the sun set behind mounting crowns of smoke shouldering up from neighborhoods far from here and rose again above the lake and the glittering Oz of the city center where stooges in suits—our own families some of them—persisted in shifting numbers from one column to another and believed it somehow still mattered. When I never had to worry about tampons or pads because that shit's always the last to get looted and for blocks all around stretched a smorgasbord of everything a prudent soul could want. When it was freedom to drink stolen booze and eat stolen food and freedom to talk all night without care for morning or care for fear or care for the electricity that was out and may or may not ever come back on. Freedom to watch the kaleidoscopic dance of the horizon's glacier of fire and admit today's apocalypse was actually pretty neat. Freedom to make a fire in the yard because it feels good to indulge in fire. Freedom to avoid the populated parts in preference of sifting like rats in the trash and freedom to burgle spray paint from a burnt-out hardware store so the lacquerheads we knew could go nuts tagging our bedrooms and windows and hissing fresh murals on our walls, our lawn, the street out front of our home. Freedom to meet strangers and love them for a night and never see them again and freedom to feel okay with that choice. Freedom to crouch behind the furnace in the cellar to smoke dope with Hannah because it's always more fun getting high when you're hidden. Freedom to rainy-day wrestle Denver in the mud of our yard and make him eat the lawn. Freedom to strut mons-first through life. Freedom to remember and not ache with what I remember. Let the sun take the blame for it. The freedom of thermal gain. I'm free in this moment to remember without fear of suffering for what I remember. That first summer of liberation and squalor, free from knowing who we were or what we'd become. No one yet dead or strung out or disappeared or run away. No one yet denied this warming light. In this warehouse where no one is meant to be, among rafters and rats and stained muslin and plated glass, within the tang of black rubber sliced and sun-baking on the floor, I can bask in the light and be free from the basic bruise of missing my friends, can be free to simply remember and remember gladly. After all, isn't that the point of everything I've built like a cathedral to surround me here? The freedom of being invited into the space where I want to be. The freedom of never having to leave.

PERIPHERY

THE FIRST house we occupied was two stories of buttercream Craftsman in a south-side neighborhood that had recently been under attack but now was pretty chill, most likely due to just about everyone having fled to safer terrain (whatever that might mean for whom). There were derelict houses and burnt-out tenements and shops bombed flat for blocks all around, but our house had nearly all its windows and the blackened carcass of a car out front and, in the yard, an old tipped-over fridge kinda partway sunken into the ground that, when we opened it, a little girl in a flower-print dress jumped out of, screamed in our faces, and ran away, black pigtail braids flapping against her retreating back. Thus absconded our last and only neighbor. And that was okay. The fewer opportunities for us to be seen, the better. That's why we were here and not downtown where everyone had jobs and worries of property devaluation. There were no packs of stray dogs rooting in the rubble for dinner and the smell of fresh death didn't hang like a fog all over, so really, what was there not to love? The house had a goofy assortment of mostly useful furniture and family pictures on the walls and running water but no electricity. But what did we need electricity for? It was summertime. We took for granted the light when we had it and used the dark when it came, TC and Denver and Hannah and I and whoever else wanted to flop and party and forage and make art with us. In a part of the city all to ourselves, we had a castle. Kids accountable to only one another. While the baby-dick police lorded around as if everyone was an enemy and the resistance fighters mortared whoever they were that day resisting, we were founding a vagabond empire, fleet footed and beholden to no one. The shittiest utopianeers: we were kings.

WHEN THE lawn-fridge (which, as I recall, was torched black all over its white-enameled shell like a tooth discovered after a fire) yawned open to belch forth the little girl-child in a leaping fit of runaway screams, Denver (who'd been the one to pry open the door's rust-stiff locking handle and was thus closest to the unexpected bursting out) understandably sprang backward—legs pedaling like a cyclist in reverse—nearly tripping over the slush-grey tails of his trench coat, his eyes alight not with shock or surprise but something closer to glee. Which makes sense. It makes sense to me that Denver would like finding a girl trapped in a fridge. Contrast that with Hannah, like a snowman's high-speed melt, slumping in a tired kind of defeat so that her supple knees knocked together and her backpack slid off her shoulder to the grass. Her little involuntary laughs, I remember, were just this side of breathless. TC, however, was fine, remained unflap'd, as if our new home's salutary absurdity—indicative of the barely coherent chaos abounding all around—couldn't possibly touch the composure steady at his core. Like: of course our lawn has a refrigerator. Of course that fridge has a child inside. Where else would a child be? What else could a fridge contain?

OR MAYBE more accurately put, we were bandits who by and large nobody cared enough about to notice, let alone stop. Which, when your dominion is only yourself, isn't any different than royalty. When we were done with that house, likely all the next occupants would see fit to do would be to wreck the sheet-rock, extract all the copper, and move on. But this was our home. We slept there and felt safe asleep. On the stairway wall hung a hokey-ass box-store tapestry of a buck standing in a glade or some shit, a piece of machine-made kitsch I would stare at for hours, in awe of the creature's lopsided eyes staring into some vague middle distance or maybe just staring at the tip of its own nose. The previous inhabitors had sincerely loved this thing, had bought it and tacked it to their wall. Now it was ours. Their sincerity became ours too. The backyard had a rope swing I more than once shared with a new and passing partner and the front yard turned into a soupy pit each time it rained, sinking the tipped fridge a little deeper with every storm. Sometimes Denver and TC would take turns inside it, competing to see how long each could remain locked in its coffin dark before freaking out. Denver always won. But the game proved them both to be ass-holes. Each would always wait a second too long before letting the other out.

Take a moment to imagine yourself inside:

Fit yourself within its hollow, knees folded and cocked to the side, back pressed into the plastic inner shell.

See the inside of the still-open door, its narrow shelves and specialized compartments reserved for life-giving things.

See the sky above, blue or cloud-swept or deepening toward black with the violence of an imminent storm, its threat heavenly and directly above.

See the door swing shut overtop you, its handle locking loud and fast into place.

See the darkness, total and best known by things fit to be consumed.

Try and count your breaths.

Try and count the seconds before the calm remnants of your reality crumble into panic.

Fuck that. I never dared take them on with their Desperate Fridge Challenge. It's doubtful I could even have stood for them to drop shut the door (for most people, I suspect, reclining in an open casket should be death-thrill enough). But that was a long time ago. These days, I'm positive, neither of them would stand a chance.

IN KINDA the same way I find it helpful to now and again remember the names or at least the faces of the women I've had the great honor of fucking, I think it's useful sometimes to bring to mind all the places where I've slept. It brings an order and focus to all the other memories that on their own tend to float in a timeless ether. As if my beds are the tethers that make every other stupid thing I've done fall into some kind of sense.

And by places where I've slept I don't mean, like, on the Red Line late at night with my whiskey-steeped brain conked against the glass or anyplace else I might've nodded off for a minute or two. Nor do I mean the beds of strangers or the pieces of rug or floor claimed for a single night or a couch or the back of a car or, just once, an especially wide windowsill. No, I mean *my* places, the specific locations I meant whenever I said I'm going to bed. Like my bedroom growing up or the dorm room I billeted in for four years straight without a single roommate: my *stuff* had to have been there with me. The few weeks before occupying the buttercream Craftsman when I roosted on Lily's couch and her living room was my *de facto* bedroom and we'd sometimes—in the worst of those inexplicable solar-flare May days that made August look like a balmy pussycat of a March afternoon—take all the food and all the shelves out of the fridge and sit inside because even smooshed together it was the coolest room in the house. My room at the buttercream that the lacquerhead geeks had completely covered in graffiti and then later my room in the Queen Anne townhouse and all the nights I stayed at the Pigeon Queen's that, if tallied together, probably equaled months of my life. The hangar bay by the lake and my cramped-ass mechanical room. Our cupola'd bungalow. Our warehouse by the river. The couch in TC's studio. The studio I now call home.

Seems like there should be more, though. As in, that can't possibly be enough beds to make up an entire life, can it? It's as if there are numbers absent from the set: I suspect a thing's missing somewhere between these brackets.

———

BUT I guess that's the risk that's run—the perdurabilities of masculinity and friendship tested side by side within the crypt of a musty blast-scored fridge—when boys crush on Chris Burden or any other asshole eager to nail himself cruciform to a Volkswagen Bug or make a performance of his adultery. (Then again, who am I to judge? I'm the one, after all, who Lawrence Weiner'd herself into believing that *thinking* about art was enough to make one an artist.) I wonder if ever while out in LA, TC itches to trap someone in a box. I wonder how often Denver on his own finds a way to remain shut up in the dark.

As far as I know, neither ever asked the other to put a bullet in him. Though of course, there's more than one way to pull a trigger.

IT WAS fun making new friends after the university got bombed. Marlene was a photographer we knew or anyway came to know, though the consistent glamour of her carriage and dress would at a glance suggest that she was more comfortable in front of the camera than behind it. Honestly, it was almost a little too much. The gold sequins. The ruby on one ring finger and the sapphire on the other. The perfect coiffure. The black Nat Shermans fitted one after another into an actual long-stemmed ivory holder. Who can do laundry in such a getup?

Now given such a public face, one would expect (or at any rate, be vulnerable to such clichéd thinking as to expect) that Marlene would work in fashion, but she was actually an arts documentarian (mostly). I came to know this one night when Denver and I were throwing back drinks at a dark back table at the Oral School, which had undergone quite a reversal in image and clientele over the course of just a year or so, somehow now appearing posh to the eyes of the slicker drinking crowds despite the pock-marked bar and stain variegation on the floor. Perhaps some cultural cachet—Blitzkrieg Chic, let's call it—had been bestowed due to its proximity to the bombed-out campus. Meaning the scarred and beer-sticky tables were crowded now with brokers and closers, corner-office holders and secret fraternal handshakers. Even still, the staff recognized us as the firebomb survivors and, as such, treated us with a veteran's respect, despite our loosened ties and open blazers donned so as to blend in with the surrounding Hump Day financiers washing their worklives away with domestics and Red Bull cocktails (our workdays, of course, were just beginning). In his typical mannish love of theatrics, Denver thrilled in this small play of dress-up, in the simplicity of hiding in plain sight, but this was to a degree how I dressed anyway: a little too fancy to be casual and a little too sweated-through to be respectable. Which meant I wasn't really hidden at all. Most of the abounding douches probably mistook me as some kind of intern or fresh-faced college whelp, perhaps even Denver's sweet-cheeked protégé, working for nothing and showing it despite my efforts. It's possible I assume too much what others assume of me. But somewhere around our second round, Marlene appeared and joined us at our corner high top, looking like the singer in a jazz club and parsing the room with just as much sensual grace. While Denver and I carried on with whatever pedantic whiskey ramble we were on, Marlene smoked two cigarettes to bookend her one rye Old Fashioned and barely said a word. Or at least no word I can recall. I remember, her eyes were Cool Hand Luke blue. Just devastating. For some obscure and animal reason, I wanted to see her teeth. But she never once smiled enough for that. When she plucked her second Nat Sherman from its ivory stem and dropped it in the ashtray, Denver gulped the rest of his drink, paid their tab, and followed Marlene out the door and into her car: they were heading up to Denver's lakeside studio to photograph his current series of creep-ass sculptures. But I was used to such abrupt exits. I finished out the night chipping some suit's front tooth for calling me a dyke, then went back to the office mechanical room I was temporarily occupying (this being the period between the Queen Anne townhouse's evicting electrical fire and our occupation of the cupola'd bungalow), cold-water washed my face in the utility sink and got back to frittering over whatever I thought I was making back then.

Marlene never photographed any of my work, if only because I wasn't producing anything at that point that could meaningfully be caught on film. And I couldn't tell you how many of my friends' portfolios she shot (though if I were to guess, I'd say pretty near all of them). In truth, I only ever saw her really at work once, when I was lung-sick and crashing on the couch in TC's studio and she came to document his paintings. Her setup seemed really antiquated to me, but what the hell do I know about cameras and lighting? Pretty much all my experience in the medium has been limited to some form of street photography, none of which I've actually conducted myself. She and TC erected his big, heavy paintings one after the other and adjusted the lights and after five hours or so, they were done. It somehow struck me as an oddly swift process and also a lot of real labor, less like the goings on of two artists and more like a master technician—a surveyor or architect—and her apprentice diligent at their job. Marlene was surgical in her adjustments, efficient in her movements. Even her smoking seemed disciplined in its control and gesture, like some weird monk in meditation. She only dropped her ash when she wanted to. It all stood in such stark opposition to her sparkling black gown, the shimmering tiara in her hair.

In those years I knew Marlene—while I gradually transitioned out of the crust-punk squatter lifestyle and into something a bit more stable if not equally squalid—she and I were almost never alone together. I'm not sure I could even repeat a single one of our conversations. Each time I try, all I see are those impossible Paul Newman eyes cutting through the smoke-thick atmosphere of a bar or a house party. How is it that it always seemed like we were locking eyes in silent concord amid all the raucous macho boys who made up our social circle? How did her gaze seem to contain so much knowledge, convey so much meaning? And did any of this ever actually happen beyond the arena of my fantasizing mind?

Only once did Marlene and I ever make arrangements to meet out, just the two of us, which proved to be the first of only two times I ever saw her in the full light of day. We met for coffee on a Tuesday or something at some anonymous kind of cafeteria—I remember, in her black high heels and pencil skirt, she was the most conservative I'd ever seen her—and even though she'd contacted me, had something she wanted to discuss with me, I couldn't tell you what we talked about or if we talked at all. I remember at one point she was asked by a busboy to put out her cigarette and her singular look of shame as she tabbed out her smoke in a saucer, remember how the whole time, she kept her blue eyes low.

I wonder now, though—within the insulating caul of thermal gain, illuminated glass and the geometry of light the glass arrays—how possible it is that this is all Marlene really wanted to show me. That she was vulnerable. That she was capable of being shamed.

It was nearly a year before I saw Marlene alone once more. Again, it was daytime. Again, she called me. Most of our boys by then had in their own ways dissolved into the teeming anonymity of the world, snatching opportunities in safer cities or rural outposts where no one knew their true names, or otherwise caught in crossfires or mortar barrages during any number of brief and unexplained upsurges of violence between the city and whomever that day had a complaint and means of making it heard. But I suspect that even if TC and Denver and the rest of them had hung around, I still would have been the one to whom Marlene reached out. From opposite ends, we'd arrived at the same place. Since I had finally gotten enrolled on some sort of federal aid—a bureaucratic impossibility had it not been for TC's intervention, which incidentally proved to be his last act of compassion before vacating my life for good—and as a consequence didn't have to hold down one awful job or other that I'd eventually get fired from anyway, I was free to meet Marlene when she called. I walked to her apartment and knocked on the door and she answered in a worn-out silk nightgown, threadbare and dirty. Her skin was skim-milk blue. And she was bony. There was even a faint Prussian shadow of stubble coarsening her sharp chin and cheeks. That, more than anything, is how I knew she was sick.

This was the last time I'd ever see Marlene. You'd think I'd remember what we talked about. We drank Nescafé at her small Formica table and smoked cigarettes and I guess had to have said something. But what I remember are her walls, whitewashed and mostly bare but for a couple poster-sized prints of her photographs, children playing in vacant lots or alleys or rooftops or tenement basements. Her apartment was one big room with a bed and a table and a kitchenette and almost everything else dedicated to her photography. I remember, her old-looking camera—positioned before a light-diffusing neutral drop—dominated the room like a throne or altar, the capturing mechanism she worked through her devastating blue eyes. The air smelled of vetiver but also of something sour underneath. The Formica was blue and pocked. The chairs were of matching leather and chrome. But I cannot remember one word we said. When I first arrived, I administered a shot into her left arm because she was too shaky to hit the vein herself, and I could not say then or now if I was shooting her medicine or dope or if at that point there was even a distinction. I withdrew the syringe and in a moment her wavering hands calmed. Then she boiled water in an electric kettle and we had our Nescafé.

Before I left, Marlene had me stand in the lacuna between her camera and the neutral backdrop on the far wall. Then she took my picture. There was a particular sort of intimacy in that, knowing her eyes were on me in a different way, that she was looking at me through the tool of her perfection, her most rarefied self. She was seeing me as best she could and maybe seeing me at my best as well. It made everything in me feel afloat. It's possible I reflected that buoyancy in my pose. Then the camera clicked, and it was done. At her door, she held me in our silent goodbye and immediately I was aware that this was the only time we'd ever touched. I could feel her heart unsteadily working behind the brittle weave of her breastbone, feel her hot breath on my ear. But of course, that one photograph was our real intimacy.

A few months later, I heard that Marlene's family had claimed her body and buried her in a suit behind their church somewhere in Pennsylvania. The name ground into her tomb-stone was Marcus. I'm sure, in their zeal for appropriateness and correction, her family trimmed away every curl and lock of her gorgeous golden hair, sculpting what was left into a pomade part. In all I've seen and all I've experienced, this might be the greatest act of violence I can recall. The people who claimed to love her most, at her most vulnerable, stripping her of her iden-tity and hiding her in the grave of a boy.

I suppose it's too obvious to say I never saw that one por-trait she took, never saw how Marlene's eyes really saw who I was and am.

———

A RAT is moving somewhere around me. I can hear it when I pause in my work—to measure a bolt, to suck a glass splinter from my thumb—though where in this warehouse it is, I can't say. Maybe in the converted bathroom? Splashing in developer? Nesting in abandoned contact sheets?

I'm not going anywhere near that thing.

BUT NO, it hadn't been a pedantic whiskey ramble. We were discussing Eva Hesse's *Accession V*, Denver and I, while Marlene silently listened in the Wednesday night din of the Oral School. We were debating which was more impressive, the monumental alien beauty of the sculpture (monumental, despite being an open cube of only 10" × 10" × 10"), or the reality of its construction, its physical process, tightly hand-knitting hundreds of black rubber tubes through the unerring grid work of holes bored through the container's corroded-steel planes. So many years past, I can't tell you which of us took what side: arguing was just a way to dig deeper into our appreciation of the gorgeous, inspiring vessel Hesse had constructed—her nimble fingers, her nimble mind—just years before her too early death. What I do remember, though, is the joyfulness of our argument, how we each kept dredging up details from our memory (the tubes' cut ends creating a bristling interior like a geometric hairy mouth, the outside's uneven oxidation creating the impression of an orange cloudscape of rust beneath the arching tubes), all while Marlene's glacial eyes appraised us, all while Denver—with the delicate finesse of an Ottoman miniaturist—unwrapped packet after cellophane packet of saltines, balancing the square planes of soup crackers on edge to construct a palace of open cubes balanced atop open cubes. We were drinking and carousing in a loud and bustling barroom, and somehow calm at its center, Denver's hands—entities independent and distinctly willful—executed a geometric tribute to equilibrium and patience.

I've always envied that. The ability to be two things at once.

Too soon, of course, it all had to end. To make a point, Denver mentioned something about Sol LeWitt, and from her quiet redoubt at the table's edge, Marlene pursed her lips, blew a thin stream of smoke through the chambers of his castle, and announced that Sol LeWitt was a slick and fussy false Italian. That's when she finished her drink and dropped her second black cigarette in the ashtray. Denver finished his drink too. The time had come. They rose and they were gone, moving on to the task of photographing Denver's sculptures—the business of making art about art—and leaving me alone in a room full of strangers while wisps of blue smoke still curled out from the apertures of Denver's creation.

FACT IS, all the photographers I knew back in that era of festival and squalor were women. Marlene and Lily and Hannah. While the boys painted their enormous canvases or welded scrap-metal obelisks or composed twelve-hour minimalist operas, drinking and talking and drinking, these three women took a step back and watched, then later developed what they saw in the dark.

Other women moved about in our circles too, of course. Painters and sculptors and drinkers and talkers. But I find it strange that on the whole, the men I knew avoided photography completely as a medium, some even going so far as to forego— and even outright prohibit—documentation of their work, oftentimes claiming as their own Robert Irwin's assertion that photographs contain nothing that the work is about and everything that it isn't (an especially bold claim for some of these idiots, whose work clearly demonstrated it was about absolutely nothing). Although maybe it's not so much strange as fitting. After all, it's one thing to pontificate about negative space and eminence and development, yet it's something else altogether to embrace such abstractions as a discipline and render them concrete. Which in so many ways strikes me as integral to the experience of being a woman, where eminence and development are not abstractions, our negative space anything but negative. But maybe I should skip the generalizations and just say *my* experience.

Of these three women, only Marlene ever took my picture and only Lily ever shared with me her bed and even that was just the one time. She was blonde and slight and looked like an office girl from a Capra movie but worked almost exclusively documenting the city's BDSM culture—of which none of us were sure if she ever took an active part (assuming, that is, you consider observation a passive act)—but in her broom-closet-sized bedroom in the Pigeon Queen's shambling wreck of a house, there hung only a single image and not even a photograph but a print of a silverpoint drawing depicting Christ suffering on the cross. It's the one image I saw again and again each time I raised my face from Lily's dinner plate. The spiked-through hands and feet. The wind-ruffled INRI and serving-platter halo each above his downcast, thorn-crowned bean. The rocks like a fist holding the cross upright and the distant mountains brooding on the horizon like a sulk or a threat or both. A sulking threat. A threatening sulk. Had my mind not been elsewhere, I could have entertained myself with concocting clever profanations of the Gloria Patri or Salve Regina. As it was, I would surface from Lily's box for a breath and think: *Oh man, that dude is dead!* I would surface for a breath and think: *He lives!*

I can't remember now which conclusion I arrived at because Lily came in a flailing, hyperventilating ecstasy, eyes rolled back and gagging on her own tongue. I hadn't known she was epileptic. She hadn't warned me her orgasms and seizures often came hand in hand. At first I in my arrogance thought my oral game had finally reached the majors. Then I thought maybe I'd broken her. Not quite knowing what else to do, I wrapped myself around her so she wouldn't bust her knuckles on the enclosing horsehair walls (or, for that matter, further fatten my lip while bucking at my face), and eventually she calmed and held me back, then in a while did her damnedest to send me into fits as well. In all the chaos of gasping and thrashing, I forgot all about Jesus martyring himself for our sins above us celebrants convulsing, sweated and enraptured.

For whatever reason, Lily and I never hooked up again, though we had no shortage of opportunities. We even lived together for a time, she and Hannah and I all squatting in a vacant warehouse that somehow still had electricity and running (albeit very cold) water. This was, in fact, my specialty for a while, finding safe abandoned places where the utilities hadn't yet been cut. For the better part of a year, the three of us shared that huge, vaulting space, the two of them converting one industrial bathroom into a darkroom and stringing clotheslines all over to hang their prints to dry while I, for my part, dislodged a metal desk from what looked like a manager's office and dragged it over to one of the back arrays of windows where I could lord over my notebooks and sketchpads and stare out at the post-Trickle-Down brownfield outside and do fuck-all else. We each took up separate nests in different nooks of the warehouse, and while every other space was communal, these discrete sleeping pods were respected as off-limits. So I can only assume suffering silverpoint Jesus still watched over Lily as she slept. And while she never expressed it or even suggested such, I wonder if that's part of why we never fucked again, why I never knew of her partnering up or bedding down with anyone else before or after our (and you know, I'm not afraid to say it) spectacular lovemaking. Some vestige of Christian guilt or shame about the way she loved and lived, something puritanical in her upbringing she could not shake or maybe, in some Stockholm syndrome way, didn't want to.

Or maybe my deductions are just as clichéd and bigoted as those of any conversion therapist or armchair psychoanalyst and I should keep my stupid mouth shut (after all, I would not suffer patiently at all any fool brazen enough to theorize as to the roots of my toothsome libido). Maybe I'm not as good a fuck as I like to fancy myself. Maybe Lily simply wasn't keen on indulging her epilepsy, with or without nude company.

Regardless, Lily was the first to leave our warehouse haven, rightly citing November's killing frost as sufficient reason to find a home with heat for the winter. A few weeks later, Hannah flew home to Vieques for Christmas and, as far as I know, never came back. For two more months I cohabitated with little more than the prints Hannah had left behind, which mostly amounted to studies of industrial architecture, sterile and unpeopled. Then in February TC found me fevered and pneumoniac, gathered me up, and ensconced me on his studio couch where I eventually, after a haze of weeks, recovered. Few straight men have been so kind to me as TC (if he hadn't been the one to suggest, over shots and Schlitz at the Oral School, that we—he and Denver and Hannah and I—counter our spanking-new homelessness by finding someplace cheap or free to live together, I likely would never have discovered my knack at sniffing out safe, abandoned places, never would have grown to consider these folks as family, would in all likelihood—for better or worse—not be here today). It's more than probable that I would have died in that warehouse had he not come along when he did. Immeasurable as my gratitude is—as unpayable my debt—from what I can tell, the only emotion TC feels for it is regret for not having come check on me sooner.

In the spring when I was healthy enough to resume creeping around in the outside air, I went back to the warehouse to collect the papers I'd left behind, but in my absence the place had been inhabited, wrecked, then abandoned by skater kids. Incomprehensible graffiti covered all the walls. Used condoms and trash everywhere. Any trace that Hannah and Lily and I had been there was gone. No pages. No prints. All evidence that my friends had existed—had existed with me—reduced to anonymous scrap, biological effluvium, and one of our sleeping bags stabbed to death in a corner. Which is to say: no evidence of us at all. Even my galvanized desk was unaccounted for, replaced inexplicably with one enormous black scorch mark on the floor and, high up like a nightmare threat of sleeping bats, a matching twin on the ceiling above.

AND HERE'S a partial list of places Hannah and I would hide to get high, in the order in which they occur to me:

- In the basement of our buttercream, in a nook between the foundation wall and the cold furnace. There was a ground-level window we could open a crack to let the heady smoke curlicue out. If we'd been thinking, we could've fit a couple chairs down there too (though I admit, it was good and healthy thigh work, squatting there in the dark).

- Our makeshift attic dance studio where no one but us could find the stairway up.

- On the terra-cotta roof of our Queen Anne townhouse, where we one time simultaneously slipped from our perch on a buildup of ice and nearly crashed into the brambly hedge below (the same hedge, in fact, that Denver in a fit of self-destructive boredom would later back flip into). We sufficed to smoke-up in Hannah's room after that.

- The black rubber roof of our freshman dorm where the blue jays would always attack Hannah's hair.

- Actually, maybe too many roofs to count.

- In a pair of leather barber chairs on the back porch no one used, gazing hazy-eyed across the mortared yard behind our rental bungalow at the winter crows winging in by the thousands.

- In the airshaft of the university's glass-arts building, where we were free of diving blue jays and, like idiots, believed we were toking unseen.

- Again in the bungalow, just one time we smoked all our dope in this straight-edge kid's bedroom. He fancied himself a writer and had very serious opinions about everything and was no fun at all and totally deserved having all his shit stinking of ultra-gooey hash. He moved out soon after that.

- One more roof, the one atop the airport parking garage, watching the very few planes come and go while getting soaked in December rain.

TC HAD been working on a series of phthalo blue paintings up until the weeks I took up residence in a fevered delirium on his studio couch. Which isn't to say he quit his series once I began my emergency cohabitation with his work. I just don't recall him producing any more paintings during my stay, at least nothing in phthalo blue. But who am I to say the two events are unrelated? I mean, how often does an outside force precipitate an internal shift? After all, if he had not found and escorted me out of my warehouse squat, I would never have lost all my years of note-book work, would likely have never felt myself tugged down and suffocated by the undertow of despairing self-abnegation and consequently would never have made the decision to give up living in abandoned buildings and all the other nihilistic bullshit that went along with being an intellectual bum, including the mordant navel-gazing that I'd come to consider as—too seri-ously, to my determinant—my creative practice.

Anyway, it was these phthalo blue paintings that Marlene came to photograph while I was still recovering, wet-lunged and swimmy-brained. I remember, the medium itself posed specific challenges to their efforts to document, as each piece was painted on an 8' × 4' × 1/4" sheet of industrial aluminum I had discov-ered and TC had reclaimed from a derelict factory amid the sulfurous brownfields ranging alongside the city's southernmost river. Despite (or maybe because of—I really don't understand the refractive and reflective properties of different paints) the uniformly even application of phthalo blue, the sheets each held a distinctive metallic gleam, an aspect TC considered cru-cial to the actual, individual experience of the paintings but detrimental to photographic documentation. It was a problem Marlene was uniquely suited to solve. But it took time.

Wrapped in a blanket in a sprung wingback chair tucked into the studio's corner (sick as I was, I did not want to appear completely infirm before the glittery splendor of Marlene), I watched the two of them work, taking note of how TC nimbly set up the panels and adjusted the lights like a homunculus extension of Marlene's will as she never once cut her cool blue-eyed gaze away from the subject at hand. It struck me then how willing and enthusiastic TC would endeavor the most menial or painful task for the sake of the work and vision of whomever he in the moment was working with. And so, too, in her own steadfast way, would Marlene. The perfection and execution of the work is what mattered most. All personal concerns were secondary at best.

Because the sheet metal we'd salvaged from the long-defunct factory was old and ill kept and exposed to the elements, each panel bore a unique mark of wear and weathering and indelible grime, all of which variously showed through the layers of phthalo blue. It was these discrete imperfections in the metal's surface that gave each painting its character: while some read as dyed enlargements of biological samples on a slide, others seemed to contain monochromatic storm systems or the smear of finger-prints ruining a mishandled collodion plate. Some registered as diffuse landscapes. A few somehow even suggested portraiture. All of it the random permutations and wild vagaries of neglect.

There was one painting, though—possibly rendered from the aluminum sheet most safely nestled at the bottom of the original factory stack—that bore no visible imperfections at all. An 8' × 4' sheet of perfectly reflective phthalo blue. Of all of the paintings, this was the one that most obviously owed a debt to Ellsworth Kelly and Yves Klein both, a fact that potentially cast the whole series in a reductive, and thus dismissible, light. But for me, that painting—so clearly eminent from the color field tradition—was also the most perfect. When alone in the studio, I would stand as close to the painting as I could get so that all other visual input disappeared past the edges of my peripheral vision. I would drench my retinas in a luminous phthalo blue— nothing else in the world but phthalo blue—whose only dynamism existed completely within the changing light from the studio's external wall of glass. I would remain for hours in the thrall of phthalo blue, rendered on a piece of industrial trash that did not exist until I'd found it. I could have dissolved into that wash of phthalo blue and never have known or cared what I'd lost.

PLANE

I OFTEN dream of building a maze with the people already inside. While they stand at the center of a square white room—or, really, like some huge James Turrell internally glowing cube—I gradually elide in one new wall of black Masonite after another, partitioning space to create an ever-more complex nest of intersecting planes, constricting the people within into tighter and tighter cells where escape at last is impossible, smothering all ideas of INSIDENESS or OUTSIDENESS and leaving only CONTAINMENT, after which I am free to go about my business.

Though maybe in recent years that dream has changed. The black Masonite replaced with panels of scrim so you can see the form, if not the detail, of the planes and people on the other side. There's something between us, but we're not apart. The scrim gathers up and radiates back the clean light of the room as I glide the final wall into place, locking myself inside with everyone else, the whole lot of us safely—at last—contained.

DO WE make choices or do choices make us? Even as far back as the buttercream Craftsman we first occupied, I was compiling extensive and obtusely meaningless lists. I certainly had no idea why or to what end—it wasn't a compulsive habit, I was doing it on purpose—and even now it's dubious as to whether I know what I'm doing or what my motivations might be (as in, I cannot decide which school of thought feels closest to true, whether the more you look the more you find, or the less). My most honest guess might fall somewhere between wanting to feel as busy and creative as the rest of my friends and sensing any such task to be as uniformly futile as any other. I could fashion perfect cubes out of compressed plastic bags or long-distance run or take up arms alongside whoever the hell was laying waste to whatever part of the city was under dispute on that particular day or be a mom or learn Aramaic. Or I could make lists.

Because at my heart I am shallow as a mirror, my first list was of footwear. Never any details regarding the people attached, just the shoes themselves, the boots or sandals or pumps or clogs, the colors and materials and designs and brands taken down in meticulous, systematic detail. (One example that stands out—and I'll admit, this may at least partially be because of the lovely young woman attached to them, all enormous blue eyes and wicked pixie cut—is a pair of Nike low-tops speckled all over in black and white like the cover of a composition notebook.) It seemed important that I include no drawings or diagrams, a practice that organically carried over into almost every other list that followed: the shape of people's hands, the time and location of disembodied pigeon wings I found a little too often in the streets, all the little rivers and canals that crosshatched our city like a web of water, strollers left out (I wouldn't dare say abandoned) on the sidewalk, where and when I spotted tuna-steak grey cats (less often than you'd expect), the names and vitals of girls and women reported missing in the city papers. I'm sure I could have bullshitted some excuse as to the purity of this choice, the no-drawing rule. But truth is, I draw like a left-handed child being ruler-whipped by a nun into using her right hand. Which, in a sense, I guess I still am.

Anyway, the one exception to the rule came in the second winter after the university bombing, when TC and Hannah were each awarded state grants which in turn paid for a regular rental home (or anyway, regular despite—and consequently discounted in light of—the mortar crater dominating the back lawn). About a dozen of us in some rotation lived there in the long, squat bungalow (I mostly encamped in the haunted-ass cupola where the last residents had stapled hardcore porn centerfolds to all the exposed rafters and beams: one more thing to study and to list) through the cold months and into the spring, all on the generous sharing of the grant monies and whatever other larder we could collectively scrape together. We stocked up on free clothes from churches and shelters and learned where all the best dumpsters for foraging could be found in our neighborhood and even drew up schedules as to which days boasted the best yields from each location. It was by far the easiest winter we ever had together, something a few of us were aware enough to recognize we would never have again. In this way—even in the face of the most bitter cold—these months were a luxury. Bundled in a wealth of secondhand winter clothes, I took to long snowy walks in the mornings and before nightfall, soaking in the details of the dormant world and delighting in the cold that I knew would be dispelled as soon as I got home to my friends. It was then, on these walks, that I began my drawn catalog of trees.

To be clear, there was nothing about this endeavor that even remotely approached the scientific. So many years later, I still couldn't tell you the species or genus or even the common name of any one of the trees I've drawn (a part of me is still convinced that any tree that loses its leaves must be an ash). And my criteria for what trees to include were as arbitrary as the list-making itself: I was really just limiting myself to those trees I considered easiest to draw, namely trees that autumn had denuded, were old enough to have a recognizable form but not so old as to be gargantuan, and were endowed with a uniformly upward profile. This struck me as the easiest subset of figures to draw with a winter-numb and clumsy hand. It would be years before I realized each of these trees looked like a sort of chalice or a votary exalting praise, every limb raised in benediction to the sky.

A year later, when I got sick and had to leave my notebooks behind in the warehouse to recuperate on TC's couch, the trees were the only list I was actively still keeping (and those were mostly the sickly, bent, and in all likelihood dead trees I found sporadically rooted in the polluted landscape wherein Hannah and Lily and I lived). When that work all later disappeared, it seemed like the most concrete signal that that version of my life had passed. That's when I stopped filling my life with the arbitrary, with the tasks of collecting anything under the guise of selecting *something*, no matter how mundane. Or perhaps I'd at last come aware that the definitions and patterns of that life were extinct, that there was no longer cause or space to seek out trash to shower with my pitiful accolade. I'd gathered enough very real refuse within me, and none of that shit was worth praise. It was time to seek out something else. No more empty cups. No more celebrating a cold, ambivalent sky.

AND SERIOUSLY, is it really at all surprising that I don't like thinking of it in terms of being rescued, what with all the connotations of helplessness that word conjures up? I don't particularly think I need to parse all the reasons why either. For his part, TC was just dropping by, admittedly in part because of the week or more of subzero daily highs that had the lake and rivers completely frozen over, but partly too because we're friends and that's what friends do: they visit. So him dragging me out from my pneumoniac stupor was incidental, executed with as much forethought and fanfare as if he'd dragged me to the bar or out for a slice of pizza. Thus maybe not a rescue after all. But I'll be damned if I can find another word for it.

And too, TC almost didn't find me that day, firstly because the clotheslines of Hannah's abandoned prints bisecting the warehouse created a visual clamor, and secondly because— wrapped as I was in newspapers and contact sheets and sleeping bags—he mistook me for a ratty pile of trash stuffed into a corner. And who's to say he was wrong? Those first few days of the cold snap I'd spent bundled like a hermit and shuffling around the warehouse to keep warm, too broke to go nurse a coffee somewhere and too proud to beggar shelter from a friend. I remember, in the monotony of those deep-freeze days, I studied—sometimes like a detective and sometimes like a monk—Hannah's photographs over and over again, between my sickness and the personless austerity of her prints descending into a sublime sort of euphoria or maybe sublimating myself into a fever dream: the rhythmic steamworks of my breath marrying the joinery of factory rafters and sheet metal forms, the hollow cathedral of a grain elevator, the slag hell of a foundry. I'm really not sure when I gave up and bedded down in the corner with every insulating scrap I could find jammed around my body, as in my dreams I was just as lost still in Hannah's pictures as I had been when awake. Steam pipes and vacuum tubes. Catwalks of metal grill. The repeating geometry of roof trusses. I kept thinking I could see someone, some short and disguised person secreted among Hannah's pictures like a flaw in her eyes' perfection: *You missed someone, Hannah! There's a detail you overlooked!* But every time I zeroed in on the subject, my eyes would cross and the telling shadows would apparate, opening an egress down which that secret somebody could disappear.

And then, from outside the fugue of my photographic torpor, TC arrived, an accident of time and bodies saving me from a final narcotic dissolution into the depths of my pneumoniac catatonia. I wish I could say TC didn't have to carry me out of there, that I was able to bear my own weight in exit. I wish I could say I even really remember him being there at all. What I do recall are Hannah's pictures and my breath before her pictures. I remember rocking inside an elevated train car and thinking how appropriate it felt, the arch blue sky out the window slashing to black as we plunged into the suspending framework of a tunnel. Then I remember being propped up on the couch in TC's studio amid heavy blankets and hot water bottles while TC bent over me to spoon hot broth from a chipped diner mug into my benumbed face. Planes of blue surrounding us like fragments of a sundered, phthalo world. The scent of bullion and thyme. I snarled fuck you in a glower and reluctantly took what was given.

AS MUCH as Marlene or the Pigeon Queen or anyone else, the old man was a fixture of our roving stray-dog community as far back as I can remember. Otto, we called him, but a part of me wonders if that was his given name or just something one of us came up with or a mistake he never felt called to correct. Never one to volunteer information, Otto was more than anything an observer. If you asked him questions, he'd surely talk (he wasn't rude, after all), but somehow it always seemed like the questioner without fail would soon become the confessor. In those early nomadic days, he was the William Burrows to our *Drugstore Cowboy*. In his perpetual state of calm bemusement, he drew us in and drew us out. Considering all we had and all we lacked, his was the presence we couldn't have known we needed most. A goddamn grandfather to make us feel okay about being such blatant losers.

I remember—and this might in fact be the first time I recognized something really (by which I mean clinically) wrong with Denver—I remember this one night in our buttercream Craftsman, with all these people packed inside despite the August swelter, lighted candles on every surface flicking to make the lot of us into ghouls at a séance, and coming up from the cellar (where Hannah and I had hidden ourselves behind the cold furnace to smoke a ball of hash cut with delicious opium), I found Denver weeping in a corner of the living room while kneeling on the floor next to Otto in our comfy chair, the two of them oblivious to the other people improbably playing board games all around them. Denver was stripped to the waist and smoking two cigarettes at once, gleaming with sweat and tears and way down deep in the thrall of a truly mournful grief. It was like watching a child, inconsolable and unlanguaged in their anguish. But when I at last parsed some meaning from Denver's sobs—like, finally understood these sounds to be actual words—I realized what he was talking about was how, as a kid, he'd stolen some younger boy's yo-yo and how later, his father—Denver's father—stole that same yo-yo from him. And I don't mean he took it away as punishment: Denver's dad stole the yo-yo for himself, knocked Denver to the floor and snatched up the yo-yo, then sat in his recliner watching the evening news, absently dipping and catching the caster while Dan Rather explained what the world on that day had become. The whole thing was so profoundly stupid. Yet there was no denying the primordial loss manifest in my friend. With the evidence at hand, I would even go so far as to say that this incident—the yo-yo double thievery—was the psychic wound central to his personality. A wound now revealed and exorcised with the quiet, pipe-chewing encouragement of Otto in the comfy chair while the candles sputtered and flared and our ding-dong friends played Mouse Trap. I wish I could have witnessed what Otto said to crank open the faucet on Denver's dammed-up hurt, what phrase dropped the shroud of stability to expose the tormented ghost within. But in a moment, all that was past. Denver put out his twin cigarettes and sat glass-eyed in the candlelight's waver, staring at the unsteady nothing between shadows, then not long after stood up and escaped, still shirtless, into the night. It'd be a week before we saw him again, still half-naked and also without shoes, awash in rain and crossing the yard toward home.

But like I said, from the moment our university was fire-bombed and we each were granted honorary degrees *in absentia*, Otto was among us. He in fact was at the buttercream—comfortably plugged into our one nice chair in the living room, his little glass of clear liquor in one hand and his soap-smelling pipe in the other—when the police betrayed all our sensibilities and raided the place. For months we'd flopped there unmolested along our crusty, unpeopled fringe. All until the molestation came. While we skittered for the exits like silverfish unhidden beneath a lifted rock, Otto remained passive and unmoved by the shouts and flailing billy clubs. Who can say what transpired after we all turned tail and split like the cowardly mutts we were, but when next we saw Otto re-ensconced among us, he was unscathed and unchanged. Though he never said as much, my suspicion is he couldn't blame us for our chicken-shit behavior any more than he could blame the police for theirs. And anyway—like with Denver, like with all of us in our private con-fessional moments of shame or hurt—judgment seemed always the least of his concerns.

It's this kind of evidence that originally suggested to me that Otto was someone's former professor, a mentor with whom the affection flowed both ways. Years would pass before it became clear that, despite his dapper garb and the wise equanimity of his demeanor, he was no one's professor and in fact no professor at all. No one knew, it turns out, where he'd come from or how he'd found us. Like any other mathematical constant, Otto simply existed. One might as well contemplate the why of e or π. It's always much easier just to accept.

After our lifestyle of communal living in vacant holes dried up, the old man became a less consistent fixture of our fellowship. And really, though I call him old, Otto was likely only in his midsixties when he first appeared among us in his elbow-patched tweeds and savvy canvas satchel, animal eyes and adorable grey mustache. I have, however, over the years watched him grow into a truly old man, a little stooped and smaller still, like the moisture has vaporized clear out his skin. In the wake of our squatter years, I took to visiting Otto now and then at his rent-controlled apartment the size of a shoebox, books stacked in untrustworthy piles on every available inch of floor or table or chair and a pump organ he'd play for me though never by request and on the mantle above, a photograph of a soldier but I could never tell: was it Otto? his father? his son? or just a photo, something of a stranger he found and liked enough to keep? Again, who can say. In many ways, Otto's a cipher, a thing to appreciate silently without needing much by way of answers.

This much, however, I have learned in my visits with the old man:

- The clear liquor of reliable permanence in his canvas satchel was an unaged brandy made of cherries or maybe plums, some eastern European version of *kirschwasser* he took to sharing with me only once I began visiting him in his home.

- The untraceable accent with which he spoke may in fact belong to no place at all but to the people he was raised among in a mixed-immigrant neighborhood in Cleveland, an amalgam nonce dialect of which he was the only speaker.

- The singular subject Otto would voluntarily talk about at any length was geometry, in such a way that it remains completely unclear whether he saw the relationships between shapes in terms of architecture or the divine.

- Though I'd never seen it, I'm certain there was a cat hidden among the books.

- Despite all the above indications connoting the contrary, Otto was terrible at chess.

- When the mouthpiece clicked between his grey teeth, his pipe issued forth a startling chimney—it never once ceased to surprise me—of tiny, iridescent bubbles.

THE WINTER when we all lived together in the squat and cupola'd rental was also the winter we threw a very artsy and debaucherous Christmas party, an affair that rapidly descended into blackout shortly after our handmade/readymade version of *amigo secreto* (or, as Otto insisted on calling it, A Dwarf and a Giant). I had stitched together a notebook from a bunch of cut scraps I'd found bagged in abundance behind a print shop, a multicolored mess that immediately fell apart when I gave it to that straight-edge writer kid who only briefly orbited our circle. (I remember, as the stitching unraveled, acutely feeling the need to learn how to properly work a needle and thread.) One of the lacquerheads gave me a black canvas sack with a naked baby doll inside, wrapped in chains with its eyes X'd out (I later tricked him into heel-kicking himself in the nuts). TC gave a paper-arts girl a small square painting in metallic red and matte black, something which we later learned she sold to a private collector for several thousand dollars. In an obvious flirtation with exploding acid death, Denver had made this Giger-esque sculpture out of dead AA and AAA batteries he'd soldered into a kind of skeletal nonfigure (I can't remember who got that). Marlene and Lily exchanged photographs that none of us were allowed to see. And Hannah, from this older sound artist—a guy who lived with us for just a month or two and only because we had electricity to run his drum machines and analog synths—received a pair of old-fashioned barber chairs.

In all our years of crusty survival, those two chairs were by far the nicest things we ever owned. All red leather and shiny-ass chrome. Functioning foot-pump pneumatics. And too: super comfortable. The sound-art guy (whose name I can't remember but who had a ghostly white patch of hair at the back of his head and another in his right eyebrow) hauled first one chair and then the other into our living room from the back of his Frankenstein station wagon. All my friends applauded. My notebook fell to pieces. Then everyone took a turn spinning and reclining and pretending to be late-night talk show hosts interviewing one another from the luxury of soft, worn leather. The sight of Otto reclined and spinning among us while TC interviewed him about an imaginary tell-all memoir about the secret sex lives of our evangelical warmonger vice president might in fact be the visual highpoint of my life. He was the Groucho Marx of our silly *Dick Cavett Show*. Then some Brillo-haired skater kid with an Italian last name arrived with a bottle of Rumple Minze and a backpack full of party drugs, and the rest of the night winked out like a candle guttering in the wind.

Which is probably evidence enough that we couldn't be trusted with nice things. Despite (or maybe in light of) their uni-lateral popularity, from then on the barber chairs lived out on our back porch, gradually succumbing to the season while flank-ing the rear entryway that no one but Hannah and I ever used (the backyard sloped upward in a muddy, blasted pitch to the tree line, making it of no utility or interest to anyone: a perfect replacement for our former furnace-in-the-cellar hidey-hole). Afternoons we'd spend there—she after expending her day pho-tographing forever-stilled flywheels and the compounding matrices of factory trusses and I about to search in the wintery dusk for bare trees or pretty cats or whatever—each reclined on opposite sides of the door, silently getting high and watching as, above the bristling black of the small pine forest anchoring our neighborhood in a minor wilderness, our local murder of ten thousand crows winged across the purple sky, dissolving into the trees.

———

THE EASIEST and by far most satisfying way of infuriating the Pigeon Queen was simply to call her Mom. It didn't even need to be intentional, it could just slip out—*Mom*—and she'd completely come unglued.

NOT THAT I am in any place to judge the irrationality of fury. Proof in point: I really did resent TC for having found me half-dead and completely incapacitated in my icy warehouse hell, dragging me to safety and nursing me back to health. In all ways, I was truly grateful for him and what he'd done. Yet part of me was nevertheless royally pissed. Like, why'd it have to be him? Why TC, with his endless generosity and understated goodwill? Why not Marlene or Hannah or Lily, or even a feral nutjob like Denver or the Pigeon Queen, someone who really didn't have shit so knew the irreplaceable value of what they'd sacrifice in helping me? Why'd it have to be the straight white guy born into money, the guy who could always guarantee we'd get whatever we needed, be it a hot meal or bail or a dose of amoxicillin? Most of all, why couldn't I have saved myself?

Obviously I never shared this anger with TC, and I hope I never slipped and somehow showed it (anyway, it's hard to feel justified in nursing your ideological bruise when the object of your anger helps you to and from the bathroom, makes up a bed for you in his studio and changes the sheets every other day, fixes you up with clean clothes and medicine, all while remaining steadfastly placid and asking for nothing in return, week after winter week). But for months that kernel of hurt remained embedded in the danker grottoes of my brain, even after he found me a cheap place to live, then part-time work as a desk clerk (which didn't last long), then finally got me signed up for long-term financial aid so I could sustain myself comfortably if also modestly. Throughout my weeks of recovery and weeks of walking with TC and Marlene among the brownfields and abandon where I had previously lived, skulking like thieves into and out of deserted factories: a foul little canker I could secretly, guiltily suck on like a stinking abscess tooth. It wasn't until his sister died late that summer and he trained to LA to settle her affairs, a process that beyond all reason dragged on for months and then a year and then finally into an undifferentiated eternity as TC quietly dissolved into a new life on the ocean's edge: only then did I let my petty resentment go. But shit, I knew as soon as he left that he was never coming back. Already I could see like the glacier of fire smoldering on the horizon that soon and inevitably it'd just be me: with Hannah home in Puerto Rico and Denver disappeared, the Pigeon Queen's house up in flames and Lily taking refuge in the protected normalcy of suburbia, who was there left but Otto and Marlene and me? And it's only a logical eventuality that an old man and a queen at last take leave of this unforgiving existence, leaving me at last alone in our city flush with ghosts, all of whom at one point had saved me. So I forgave TC. I forgave them all. It was their right to disappear. I'd have done the same, too, if I'd been smart enough to know how. I taxied with TC to the train depot and saw him off, knowing he'd never be back whether he knew it himself or not. Then I walked the endless blocks, crossed the limitless bridges home, and taught myself how to get used to always being the one left behind.

THE PIGEON Queen's house—and I cannot stress enough the supreme lack of hyperbole in this assessment—was a derelict Gothic Revival mansion on the mud-sliding banks of the city's more northern river. From what I can gather, this stretch of waterfront was once a single long strand of Victorian houses, nearly all of them the hedged and gated estates of shipping magnates of the previous centuries. But with the neglect and lassitude of time and generations, the merchant families fell to squalor and so, too, did the houses, which at the nadir of poverty were sold off or razed for the installation of new factories and public works depots—mountains of asphalt, mountains of sand—but even eventually those too went away, razed or abandoned and forgotten among so much poisoned earth and concrete ruin stripped of all use, interrupted only by the Pigeon Queen's sole smog-stained house like a dirty nose thumbed in the capitalist face of progress.

I never lived in the Pigeon Queen's house the way many of my friends did off and on throughout the years. I did, however, on occasion have cause to stay the night. That one time in Lily's bed. Another time on the carpet in a backroom with a touring agender Stroviolist, the morning after which they disappeared for good. But mostly just a random night here and there, on a couch or corner of floor after a party and having nowhere better to go. Because—despite its distant remove from all populated corners of the city, despite its filth and its haunted beauty—this was a place for gathering. Walking unannounced through the Pigeon Queen's door, you were just as likely to find a dozen different clutches of weirdos—goofing, blathering, high as fuck—

scattered throughout the zoo of her house as you were to find the
Pigeon Queen alone and engaged in whatever the hell she did all
day sequestered in her mildewed palace. Yet with so many
rooms—some packed to the gills with random bits of family
memorabilia and others senselessly empty—it was pretty easy no
matter the abounding circumstance to eke out some quiet privacy among the water-stained wallpaper and scuffed, discolored
floorboards. I honestly couldn't say how many nights I stayed in
that place, how many mornings I awoke to coffee and sour milk
in the dirty kitchen (the actual dining room being too clogged
with water-bloated books and leaning paper towers and decades'
worth of boxed-up tax forms), or to the sight of the Pigeon
Queen firing her rifle across the river, or even now and then to
find myself mysteriously, unsettlingly alone among all these
ghostly rooms. So despite it never being my home, I came to
know the Pigeon Queen's sprawling ramshackle pretty well.

As if in evidence of this fact, here is a partial list of discover-
ies made while roaming room to sepulchral room:

- A very outdated globe with all of Africa parceled up by its
  colonizing European occupiers, pinning down a stack of
  moisture-warped *Hustlers* on the tank of a broken toilet.

- An antique wood-and-wicker rocking cradle in the attic
  loft, backlit by a single round window and as a consequence—
  with the sharp sunbeams slicing through weightless dust—
  looking haunted as fuck.

- A black-and-white photograph of Frank Gehry's enormous
  glass fish, hanging from a nail rusting in the soggy plaster

above a different toilet, in the downstairs bathroom that among other things featured a deeply-stained wallpaper of babies and roses and ox-pulled plows tumbling in a perpetual fall.

- A small and profoundly oxidized brass statue of a Bavarian hunter—his hunting bear patient at his heel—propping open the door between the dining room and the kitchen.

- A legitimate rubber gasmask like an alien locust's heartless face, its rubber stink undercut by some other worse chemical reek, hanging all alone in the closet of a perennially unoccupied bedroom.

- An oversized and rather ungainly wooden swan that might have been a child's sleigh, centered in—what? a parlor? a drawing room?—where maybe a coffee table would have been more at home.

- Absolutely no pigeons whatsoever.

AFTER MY pneumoniac season on TC's couch, he and I and sometimes Marlene would devote entire days to wandering among the deserted warehouses and factories near my old home edging the city's southernmost river. (His phthalo paintings complete and documented while some sort of contracts worked themselves out between his agent and one gallery or another, for those few months TC had an uncommon wealth of time free to accompany my foal-legged recovery walks.) There was something Cold-War-comforting about our unrushed perambulations, all these buildings of weathered Brutalism vacant and grey with the dust of industry past, the hard blue of sky pressing down on the silence suffusing the abandon, the river's glimmering face creating the illusion of slow progress while the poisoned weeds bent colorlessly toward the cinders. Any child born in the 1970s or early '80s knows exactly what I mean: there's toddler-tall security in images like these, suggestive of safety easily found underneath any table or desk. Without a word, TC and I would stop and stare at whatever fallout shelter sign we might chance upon bolted to the corner of a warehouse or rat-ripe mill. Circles and triangles, yellow and black. Elemental with the authority of comfort.

Sometimes TC would step up close to extend a hand to the blocky yellow letters, rubbing the layered dirt away beneath his forefinger or thumb. Tracing the three down-pointing triangles within their circle of black. The pressure of his fingertips making clean these symbols within their bed of dust. Highlighting the warning anew.

Sometimes instead, TC'd throw a bottle or a rock.

If Marlene was with us, though, it'd be different. We might stop, TC and I, but she'd keep walking. The signs didn't interest her at all. Maybe she found the implied irony—that anything might be safe here—too boring to indulge. Maybe she'd already long abandoned the idea that anything could anywhere be safe.

Whatever we were doing out there—peeking through age-opaque windows, wrenching against rust-stuck doors—we weren't looking for a new place for me to live. As I said, TC had already helped me secure a studio apartment, safe and heated and virtually rent-free. No, what we were up to was more of a survey, a census of potential, to learn what these vacant structures might contain. After all, it was in one such industrial wreck that we found the aluminum panels that eventually became the basis for TC's phthalo series. It stood to reason there would be other choice finds discarded and forgotten and awaiting our discovery.

Throughout that very gradual warming of spring, though, I cannot recall us ever actually removing anything from these sites. There was a textile mill with rooms overwhelmed with bobbins of moldering thread, uncut muslin and calico and scrim stained by rain and seepage and who knows what else, monstrous looms the size of dump trucks by their physical presence alone boasting of all they once could but no longer accomplish. There was a sneaker factory with long thick mats of rubber and folds of canvas and cart after cart of unmated shoes (which I guess we did take, or anyway, I took, as these have since made up the entirety of my footwear), not to mention the ghostly piles of shoe forms like the untold severing of wooden feet. There was a glass factory terrifying in the intimate fragility of its abandoned stock, a sort of crystalline palace disassembled and laid in wait. All usable. All bursting with potential. Yet if we dragged anything out of there at the time, it's escaped my memory (like the words Marlene spoke to me the last time we met in her vetiver-perfumed apartment, like where we were when Hannah told me she had a whole bevy of siblings she'd never met from her dad's first abandoned marriage, like who it was who told me Denver would sooner sheer off his own thumbs than ask his father for help). The only real work that ever got done is when we crossed paths with the random packs of wild children and Marlene asked if she could take their portraits. Yet none of it ever felt like wasted time.

Later, as spring's pungent muck dried up and summer began making its increasingly nervous overtures, more and more I would find myself alone carrying forth these surveys along the rainbow'd skulk of the river. There was a peace to this, an airy lightness, that I could only and eventually equate to those teenage years when I got hooked on pills, then crashed, then had to get clean. Wandering among the factories made me feel like I was getting clean. And though this was the first time in years I had an actual secure home, it was also the first time—amid burnt-out relics or emptied monuments to obsolescence, the cindered lots and demented weeds and prismatic sprays of broken glass and spilled gasoline—that I actually felt *at home* somewhere. Alone in the garbagy shadow of the old, lost city. Perfectly at home. All of these things were so totally fucked up, but they could be fixed. None of it was a loss.

Sometimes, in the lengthening cast signaling afternoon's end when my hips and shoulders would deliciously ache from having spent all day afoot, I'd return to the warehouse where I used to live, stretch myself out on the scorch mark where my desk had disappeared, and watch the gold geometry of sunlight play against the leaning shadows, against the weave of trusses and the lines where walls terminated into other walls. Do you understand the freedom of resigning yourself to the futility of comprehension? To stop trying to *say* what you see and instead simply see? To open your eyes to the smoke-obscured dawn without the burdening need to explain every damn thing? This is the real liberty of the rabbit hole. I would Alice myself through the looking glass of angles, freed and lost among apertures into unseen rooms.

INSIDENESS

WHEN I was younger, a thing would happen to me in the quiet of falling snow. I don't mean when I was a kid—though yeah, probably then, too, but who cares about that?—no, I mean when I was out sketching my trees that one winter we shared a rental. The snow out of nowhere would begin to come down, and like a mainline hit, my experiential mode would change completely. All other perceptions became secondary to that universal muffling of sound. And something clean, too, the way all facts of the land grew padded out lightly in a distortion of snow. A gentle sort of chill that had nothing to do with cold would tickle up my spine like the tail of a passing cat. It would not so much paralyze me as make me long for a permanent stillness, an arrest to the violence of motion. While snow only equals accumulation to me now, for a time it demanded a delight in stillness. (That might sound like the same thing, but it's not. One is an ecstasy. One is resignation. The perpetual moreness of a condensing universe.) There was an implicit comfort in the uninterrupted obfuscation of the world, in submitting to the glaciation of everything. I wouldn't even want to sketch the naked trees I'd sought, the feeling was so overwhelming.

I would, though. Of course I would. I'd always sketch my unleafed trees. Not even the snow could put a halter on that.

Nothing can stop the violence of motion.

IN HER home, the Pigeon Queen rarely changed out of her threadbare nightgown or housedress or whatever you want to call it. You could tell, beneath the stains, it'd at one time been baby blue, though years and abuse had bleached it a slushy, purplish grey. Inside, she wore the sort of fuzzy slip-on slippers my grandmother used to wear in the winter when she felt sick. Outside—tossing food scraps into the river or shooting her gun at whatever—she wore knee-high hunting boots. Her hair was always some variation of a rat's nest.

Yet now and then, if someone was throwing a party somewhere, the Pigeon Queen would appear (always with some young and unknown lad on her arm) wrapped in a thick fur coat and her hair spun tall atop her head. Her face and nails were clean. She may even, if the mood struck, have on a little makeup. It was on those occasions that it again—and always as a surprise—became clear to me that the Pigeon Queen was in fact only a few years older than the lot of us. With her mantel of squalor shunted aside, she was overwhelmingly youthful. And gorgeous. Even when you drew close enough to notice the bald patches in her coat and where the stitching was coming undone—even when you realized her hair was simply brushed and pinned and not necessarily even clean, that under her furs were the same dirty dress and heavy boots—there was a glamour that followed her through the night.

These parties, though, were the only times I ever saw her outside the lines of her broken-down estate. Always in the batwing shroud of night. Always with an escort who could knock your fucking teeth in.

AN EXAMPLE of Otto's geometry fixation:

> *The relationship between an intersecting square and octagon (4:8) is absolutely discrete from—and in fact has no substantive connection whatsoever—to the relationship between an intersecting triangle and hexagon (3:6).*

Despite the obvious doubling (each set of ratios, after all, being reducible to (1:2) and thus, in a sense, being equal), this theory, Otto insisted, is true and provable via two simple observations. The first being empirical, that:

> *If the relationship between intersecting planes (4:8) is equal to the relationship between intersecting planes (3:6), each then would likewise be equal to the relationship between a line intersecting a square (2:4) and a point intersecting a line (1:2). Because a square is two-dimensional, a line one-dimension, and a point zero-dimensional, this would set a stupid precedent wherein the relationship between intersecting* interdimensional *forms (e.g.: two two-dimensional planes such as a square and an octagon) is equal to the relationship between similarly reducible intersecting* transdimensional *forms: a two-dimensional pentagon and a three-dimensional pyramid (5:10), a two-dimensional octagon and a four-dimensional tetracube (8:16), and so on forward and back into vapid infinity.*

The second reason being aesthetic, that:

For any given instance, the physical and emotional reactions of anyone experiencing any of the above ratios are never constant between individuals, let alone between instances, let alone between the shapes.

At which point he would demonstrate by drawing them out:

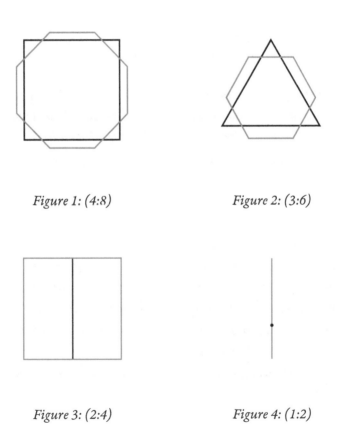

Figure 1: (4:8)   *Figure 2: (3:6)*

Figure 3: (2:4)   *Figure 4: (1:2)*

Anyone who dared argue that, the rules of reducibility extant, the relationships within these four figures of intersection *were* equal, he seemed to be saying, was a fool. So of course, who but a fool would argue? (And anyway, who was I to challenge him? I, who isn't even sure I've remembered his theorem correctly.) Just as any musician knows a 6/8 time signature is not the same as a waltzing 3/4. Because reducibility does not equate to equivalency: a glass of water, some flour, and an egg, after all, are not equal to a bowl of pasta. And having thus concluded his demonstration, Otto would revolve on his bench away from the chaos of his coffee table, face the keys, and proceed to softly play a gentle something on his pump organ. Yet in all the repetitions of this scene—and I cannot recall a single visit to his apartment that did not include at some conversational juncture this particular geometric inquiry—it was never once made clear to me: was he speaking of the relational qualities of built forms in a physical, habitable environment; the simple and primitive aesthetics of doubling equilaterals; a calculable divinity inherent in the structure of *things*; or if he even maintained between these conclusions there being any difference at all?

THE PIGEON Queen had this signature move we called The Degradator, this real assy maneuver she'd employ only in a crowded room (I guess she considered it successful only if executed before an audience). With silent guile she'd install herself behind someone (the criteria for selection were never not a mystery to me) and with one hand gently she'd grip their hip and with the other palm the back of their skull. Then slowly but with steady force, she would push against their head and pull at their hip, forcing their face down into whatever may be before them, someone's lap or a plate overloaded with food. Or maybe they'd just bend uninterrupted until their cheeks tucked between their knees. Or perhaps they'd drop into a kneel and find themselves nosing the floor. As I recall, no one ever resisted the force of her compulsion. The Pigeon Queen would maintain you in this humiliating terminus as long as she felt required while everyone else uneasily waited and pretended not to watch. Then: she'd let go, leaving you just as suddenly and pointlessly as when she'd approached.

When you're the mistress of the house, you can get away with such shit.

———

AND AS the mistress of my own house, what shit now do I allow myself to get away with? Do I roam naked through the day and flatulate triumphantly room to room? Do I let the sink fill up with dishes, then in a fit of conspicuous consumption jam the whole batch in the trash and start over with a new set, thrift-store or otherwise? Do I torture my guests with elaborate games that prove fun only for me?

No. No, none of that shit. I like my spaces clean. I almost never have guests. And I'm too stylish to squander my nudity on an empty, unperson'd room.

HIS DRAWINGS of octagons and squares—penned onto napkins, opened envelopes, the inside cover of a book close at hand—never left his squat coffee table. Otto would sketch out his demonstration of unequal equilaterals, revolve on the worn sheen on his bench, and play whatever unfamiliar organ music called to him that day. When I'd next visit, all the drawings would be right where he'd left them. Yet when the moment came, instead of referring to any one of the executed geometries littering the table, he'd sketch a new pair of octagon and square, line and point, hexagon and triangle. I guess maybe because even identical drawings of unequal equilaterals were unequal. Maybe there was something in the repetition that mattered, like the re-creation of a known form counted more than the form itself. Thus making each drawing in its own way—both a copy and an individual—precious.

Maybe he just couldn't stand to throw any of his geometries away.

IT'S ROUTINE now that keeps these days and myself within these days in a stable, even line. I have my desk and I have my coffee maker and even though this is considered an efficiency studio, I have *two* rooms to myself, a front room that's kinda big for a kitchen and a back room that's everything else with a bathroom in between, a setup that—in combination with the frosted-glass transom above each door—leads me to believe this was actually at one time an office or some other professional space. Which actually makes me feel right at home: these rooms were once meant for something else yet instead, now, there's me. I sleep and do my feeble calisthenics and futz at my desk in front of the tall, narrow windows where before some dink calculated someone else's taxes or cleaned people's teeth or assisted strangers in filing for divorce. I make my breakfast and wash my dishes where people used to sit and wait patiently for their turn at whatever while a bored receptionist half-assed a crossword and didn't answer the phone. I awake each day and do these things—stretch and box jump, boil an egg, wash up my mess and wash up myself—and if my neighbor across the hall is out (she has to travel for her dialysis), I go over to her apartment and feed her cat, Taquito, and so I know hers used to be an office just like mine. I keep my days ordered and identical inside a building of ordered, identical rooms. I perform the motions perfectly as if to prove I got this, this routine is cake. As if anyone could possibly be watching. Then, these simple maneuvers complete: I leave.

THOUGH I guess I lied before. The Pigeon Queen did not always require an audience.

Among all her rooms of random and mostly ancient shit, there was a collection of antique porcelain dolls, and when I say collection, I mean something in the neighborhood of two hundred dolls or more all arranged in a gallery neat and tidy along some floor-to-ceiling built-in shelves. Pigtails and braids and silky puffs of human hair. Sunday dresses and aprons, fur muffs and Little Red Riding cloaks. All as frippery for unblinking eyes and impassive faces, the lot of them together as if waiting to pass some frail and biased sentence in an upstairs room lit by a single yellow bulb.

I found this collection after Lily and I had slept together, and by that I mean later that same night. It hadn't been a party like most of the occasions when I fucked and passed out at the Pigeon Queen's. The evening throughout had been quiet, just Lily and me and the Pigeon Queen with whatever mute man-child she was studding that week. I had come expressly to see Lily alone. I don't know if I had arrived with the conscious intent of seducing my friend, but it seemed clear to both of us that something out of the ordinary was afoot. We sat on her bed sharing a bottle of Yard Dog Red and smoking opium from a one-hitter while taking turns trying to solve a Rubik's Cube. And when at last we had all the reds with the reds and the blues with the blues, we took off our clothes and I gave her a seizure then she brought me as close as I'll likely ever get to having a seizure, too, and after that—stoned and well-fucked—we slept, though Lily much longer than I as I have a tendency to startle awake at inopportune hours in the night and upon waking, grow restless as a stray. It's an aggravating habit and one unfair to inflict upon whoever might elect to share their bed with me. So I excised myself from the tangle of Lily and stepped into my slacks and suspenders and threadbare black dinner jacket, sneaked out the door and started to explore. Not to be nosy or anything. Just for something to do. It was too late to head home to my office mechanical room and besides, it seemed likely if I stayed the night I might score some breakfast in the morning. So I wandered in the hopes of again getting tired, foxstepping down foot-worn halls and seeing what could be seen. Which is exactly how I found myself in a creep-ass room full of dolls.

I remember, I was standing before a copper-haired Victorian princess done up in layers of calico, pondering the improbability of the Pigeon Queen owning such precious, girly things—such unlikely tokens of cloying sentimentality—when I first felt one surprise hand knitting through my hair then another clench the curve of my pelvis. I didn't need to turn to see to know who was behind me, know what was about to go down. What was already going down. Somehow, in the quiet of night, among all those rooms, she'd found me. Perhaps the Pigeon Queen sucks at sleeping too. Perhaps she knew me and my habits well enough to know to wait.

If the force of her on me had been to the small of my back, it would've been like a guiding hand leading me to dance. As it was, the intended experience was more akin to a dog having its snout pokered in shit. And believe me when I say that I cannot recall if I resisted or let her push my head down into that copper-haired doll's dusty calico lap. What I do recall, though, as I drew in the ancient smell of the doll's miniature dress, is being aware, too, of the scent of Lily still marking the everything of my face.

So really, when I think I'm remembering all those dolls arranged in the Pigeon Queen's upstairs room, that's really what I'm remembering:

- The scent of Lily's sex lingering sweetly on my hands and face.
- The perfumed scent of old clothes.
- A feeling of comfort when I knew I should feel shame.
- The feeling of a hand in my hair.

All of which really proves how ridiculous this whole memory game truly is. Who can say what we mean when we say, "I remember this person" or "I remember this one time"? Who can say what I really know when I say, "I know this thing occurred"? It casts the totality of our experience in a hued and suspect light. Which makes me wonder: What's the point of this memory of dolls and sex and power? What's the point of memory at all?

And such flawed memory at that. For after all the recalled detail and sensation, I cannot now say how long we held this pose of vulgar force and submission like a dom and her doormat stooge, cannot say how long I remained folded and owned even after the Pigeon Queen was gone.

AND SURE, maybe it's counterintuitive, but of all the repurposed fibers and strands I've gradually in my gleaning accrued, I kinda prefer above all others the bolt of calico I rescued from the textile mill. There's something very charming about how barely refined it is, how now and then I can spot flecks of remnant husk from the cotton bolls. And too, this one bolt had lain for years beneath a filthy drip from the mill's busted ceiling, leaving a blossoming stain of oil and rust and mildew repeating from one folded layer to the next, so in a Rorschach kind of way it *is* a traditional calico print. Even abandoned, it did what it was meant to do.

However. One bolt is not nearly enough. Nor is a repeating flower, no matter how disgusting, appropriate. And while it is by no means a thick fabric, it is not nearly thin enough. For example, if I were to bind my head in calico (which is absolutely *not* necessary), I would not be able to see the light streaming in through the warehouse windows. I wouldn't be able to see anything at all. Light does not pass through. It does not collect for itself the light.

Not so with muslin.

Not so with scrim.

THOUGH IT seems to me now, as I measure and hem, as I balance glass against glass, that not once have I ever recognized the music Otto played on his organ—not when he played it and not later, either, when I tried to remember the tune, when I might overhear a phrase echoing out an open church door and think *is that it?* and then think *no*—though often I've wondered if maybe he was simply, unworriedly improvising figures based only on the pleasing movements of his hands. Like, it felt good to articulate his fingers this way, and by accident, it sounded good too.

Or perhaps he was translating into music the relations between his geometries: an etude of a square transposing an octagon, a nocturne to the hexagon consuming the triangle. A left-hand melody of five notes syncopated to a right-hand melody of ten.

AND TOO, it's likely I knew exactly the Pigeon Queen's criteria, quite possibly always knew how she selected her target for shaming. Because looking back now, I cannot recall her ever once attempting to degrade anyone but me. I can easily visualize her, sure, from an outside perspective, an observer watching her crook and force somebody into the shape of her will. But what I see is a construction, a private little film of someone else experiencing what I've experienced. My face between my knees. My face in someone's mashed potatoes. I was the only one the Pigeon Queen would attempt to degrade. Even if it never worked. Even if I never felt shame so much as a certainty that it was the Pigeon Queen, not me, exhibiting such profound and public weakness. And with that certainty came power. She could try to break me. But only I could decide I was broken.

——————

YET HOW often do I mimic these poses of degradation? When I'm dragging a rake through the cindered earth? When I'm on my knees scrubbing my studio floor or inching forward a roll of rubber? When I bend to give my neighbor's cat a tasty little treat? A bit of fishy something she completely does not deserve.

OUTSIDENESS

FOR SO many years, my exclusive concern had been the finding and reclaiming of safely abandoned places. Vacated homes or office spaces, warehouses or deserted hangar bays, all outside the regular patrol of police or gangs or vigilantes scheming mortar attacks on city hall. Which is to say, free homes for me and sometimes my friends, the protecting vessels wherein I—we—could be contained. Yet it was within these derelict rooms that I squandered away years feigning work and producing nothing. I may as well have spent my twenties playing solitaire in a derelict shoe factory or textile mill, convinced I was the only thing safely enclosed inside. It took me way too long to awake to the potential of where I'd chosen to spend my days, of what else my enclosures contained.

NOT THAT I am in any position to critique even the most derivative or shallow artist—nor, for that matter, can I at all defend picking on a celebrated dead guy—but all that notwithstanding, the only thing of value I can see Salvatore Dalí having ever created was the *name* of his painting *The Persistence of Memory*. And I'm not saying that to be snarky or petulant: it's a perfectly concise definition of lived human experience. Aside from the extreme agnosiacs and amnesiacs, who among us could deny this as being their central infirmity, chronic and with no cure?

When I first kinda blanched in embarrassment at the sight of all those droopy clocks—speaking more of the artist's barely concealed impotence than anything else—then learned and consequently became enthralled by the piece's plain-speaking title—so much like a koan, ineffable yet undeniable—I understood the literal persistence of memory to be that pervading sense of haunting or hounding, the inability of any person to let go of or desist from the perpetual rereading and reediting of how things should have been, words said or silenced, actions taken or withheld. But that, of course, is how a child understands our capacity to remember and consequently laments: a teenager damning herself for whatever perceived opportunity was presented yet lost. It is not a wrong interpretation of the facts, but neither is it the only interpretation. Because I see now that this persistence has less to do with *us* and our almost obsessive self-flagellating need to recall and in fact has everything to do with memory itself, how it comes willful and unbidden into every conscious moment, impressing itself on the present. We're not obsessed with the past. The past is obsessed with us.

I mean, here I am spending my days sheering lengths of fabric into veils 438-inches long and tempting vertigo while balanced atop steel beams made creepy with last century's bubbly coating of spray flame retardant and literally risking my very limbs balancing plates of glass so much bigger than myself, yet all this time I am thinking about Hannah and Otto, about TC's phthalo planes and Lily's silverpoint Jesus, about waking up in the Pigeon Queen's house in the crepuscular predawn hours after a party and finding myself all alone, wandering from room to musty room in the half-hungover search for anybody until finally, just as the first mochi glow of daybreak showed its horizon's edge, sighting through the fingerprinted window above the kitchen table Denver outside and taking a knee by the river's frost-mud edge, tossing plates of china high into the air over the sludgy water so the Pigeon Queen in her stained housedress could blast the dishes into ceramic dust with her .30–.06 as Marlene, dressed in gold, captured it all with her antique-looking camera while the scalpel's edge of November wind sliced in from the bay.

To what end do these unbidden memories come? To what advantage do they serve my unthimbled finger and thumb?

To no advantage and to no end. It does nothing for me, this remembering.

Because it is not about me. It's the memory that demands I remember.

And with all this teeming so tenaciously in the forefront of my mind, occupying such coveted mental space, how—with what quality—will I later remember these present days of work? Will I remember these glass slivers sunk into my nail beds, the cold ache in my fingers and endless hours of hemming through a fog of other hours, other days, memories like stacked photo negatives compressing time to a single point of density and indistinction? Will I even remember what I was remembering while doing these things with my active hands and wandering mind? Or maybe the real question is: How can we possibly remember the rapidly transpiring NOW when so preoccupied with remembering the perpetuating mudflats of THEN?

I **WAS** with Hannah the day our school was firebombed by, well, whoever was doing the bombings that week. We were skipping our Philosophy of the Arts class (something we admittedly should have knocked out our freshman year but had, like children, delayed until our very last semester) because our teacher was out with strep throat and all the sub did was play Sister Wendy videos. Don't get me wrong, we loved Sister Wendy and in fact had watched the totality of her *Story of Painting* and *Grand Tour* series on our own a million times, but still, without even the ghost of an idea as to how we'd spend our time (because clearly we weren't going to our studios to burn through the rapidly dwindling hours before our looming senior shows and theses defenses came crashing unpityingly upon us), we were convinced we could idle the hours away more productively on our own. Which ultimately meant that in the late morning of the first truly warm day in April, we were on the hillside overlooking the campus—unknowingly positioned primely to witness the show to come—a little bit high and working out the rules to this collaborative project wherein I would write musical scores as translations of Hannah's photographs. The idea was that certain elements of each photograph would correspond to a coded musical notation, changes in tempo and tone and that sort of thing. The same way a Homeric poem could be reimagined as a *trompe l'oeil* or a book adapted to film, we were certain any art could be translated into new, discrete art. All we needed to do was do it and do it well. The actual performance of the music, of course, wasn't important as neither of us knew how to play an instrument (and too, we were both—I maybe more so than Hannah—enamored at the time with the Lawrence

Weiner notion that an artwork doesn't necessarily need to be *made* in order to exist). No, it was the translation between media and perceptual organs that interested us. All we needed were the ground rules—like which direction to read the image—and we could begin. It was these basic rules, the point of access into the actual work, that we'd been arguing over since sophomore year.

If we divide each image into equal quadrants, I argued, then it wouldn't matter which direction the image was read. Each quadrant would be its own statement or question or whatever, a sentence, altogether creating a sort of thematically complete paragraph.

While we spoke, Hannah sat with a sketchpad open on the easel of her lap, making shaded angles and curves with a set of primary acrylic sticks. I was lying on my back, fingering my navel through a space between the buttons of my secondhand oxford.

Okay, sure, she said. But how is that any different than just reading the whole image as a single thing? Each quadrant would just be a smaller image to read, right? You'd be translating four images—and incomplete images at that, just fragments of a whole—instead of just one complete thing.

From where she sat in relation to the sun, the dark coils of her hair glowed an earthy orange.

And you'd *still* need a consistent starting point and direction, right?

She kinda had me there.

And why quadrants? It seems so arbitrary.

It *is* arbitrary. I sat up on my elbows to better admire the glow of her hair. Quadrants are just an easy access point for divisibility.

Below where we roosted like hens on the hillside, the Financial Aid Office's windows blew out in billowing curtains of flame.

Easy is the enemy of creativity, Margaux.

Then the thunder of the blast reached us.

Maybe we should let the composition of each photograph determine the starting point and path, I said, waiting for the smell of smoke to reach us. You know, trust the work itself to be its own guide.

Now the Admissions building next door was burning too. Great puffs of grey and black poured from the shattered doors of the provost's miniature and overwrought castle-*cum*-office.

How is that any less arbitrary?

There it was: the acrid, ashy stink, overwhelming our own bouquet of sweetly citric smoke.

It's not arbitrary at all if you do your job.

I wonder if I'm really seeing what I'm seeing.

It took me a second to realize she wasn't being catty in response to my cattiness. By now, all the administration buildings on campus were exploding or on fire. There were whistling things falling, too, from the sky, like fierce little meteors that in later weeks and months I'd come to recognize as mortar shells. Things were getting increasingly serious down there. So much cackling fire and smoke. So many screams. The academic buildings and dormitories, though, seemed mostly unscathed, the one exception being the campus carillon, which had become a wildly lapping tongue of flame (we'd later learn in the Partisans' official public statement that this was an accidental casualty). For some reason, the flaming tower surreally rang "Bridge Over Troubled Water."

All this I witnessed as if through some vapor or projected on a screen. I knew these things could happen—were happening more and more—but hadn't yet seen it for myself. I didn't know it could happen to me. Us. Anyone whose face I knew. I guess I still didn't think it could happen. Even as it was happening. Even as I watched.

Do you think we should go down there? I asked. I was really hoping she'd say no.

I don't know, she said, scratching the tip of her nose with an acrylic. Seems like everyone else is trying to get away.

She was right. I could see them now, students and teachers and whoever else running like idiots in any direction they perceived as being *away*, sometimes fleeing one fire only to round a corner and find another blazing in their path or getting showered with dirt and rocks as a mortar turned a grassy swath into a hot crater. It struck me that the school should have implemented some kind of emergency protocol, a set procedure everyone was mandated to learn at freshmen orientation. But then I remembered that I had skipped orientation to face-fuck my RA while my dad's valet setup my new room down the hall, so really, I had no point of reference for my criticism. Fact is, if I were down there instead of up on the hill, I'd have been just as manic and stupid-looking as anyone else.

I hope they don't torch the Hillel House.

Hannah had a room at the Hillel House. Somehow, this Puerto Rican girl passed unchallenged as Jewish. While obviously neither of us wanted what was happening to devolve into a pogrom, mostly neither of us wanted to see Hannah suddenly without a home (we really hadn't comprehended yet the full scope of what we were witnessing, hadn't yet realized or embraced our liberation theory of squatting and gleaning). I admired that she didn't allow any suggestion of altruism in her statement to disguise her necessary self-interest: it's the sort of thing most people would deny, as if a moral abstraction could ever be more immediate than basic personal need. But I guess at this point I'm just speculating out in left field.

Are you sure that was just opium we smoked? I asked. Usually opium made me want to put together jigsaw puzzles or reassemble broken things, like I could suddenly see the hidden patterns abounding.

You mean, just opium in the hash?

(I seriously one time put back together a smashed saltine, crumb by tiny crumb.)

Yeah, exactly. Was there anything other than opium in the hash?

It had me wondering what kind of hidden patterns might underlie this firestorm and panic sweeping campus. Because so far, I hadn't seen anything revealed yet. No underlying logic and no suggestion of order. Which meant everything this day had become was little more than a senseless carnival of pandemonium. Which was more than my opiated brain could accept, let alone comprehend.

But Hannah didn't answer me. She was making like she was getting ready to leave.

What are you doing?

I'm going to go.

What, to help?

No—

(and I could clearly see it shaping her face, her contempt at my stupidity, caustic and unblemished despite the acrylic smudge pinking her nose, and somehow I knew right then I'd never succeed at composing a single melodic phrase from any of Hannah's photos)

—to the bar.

Which made sense. Which as a matter of fact was obvious. The only obvious, sensible thing happening in the world right then. Anyone we knew who was surviving this shit would eventually head to the Oral School to share names and tally the dead over well whiskey and Schlitz. We'd have assembled there regardless of the day or its events. Looking back, the Oral School was the precursor to and trying grounds for our imminent shared homes, the space that allowed our community to take up space with pride. So of course that's where we'd end up, even if Hannah had said nothing, even if we'd headed out instead for the Colombian bodega I liked (whose *piña y jamón* empanadas were all I ever wanted to eat those days) somehow, the Oral School is where we would eventually land. Who were we to stand in the way of the inevitable? It was all of eleven-thirty in the morning and it was time for us to have a drink. While property and financial records flared into equalizing flame below, we gathered our things and headed downtown to a choir of sirens and screams, thirsty and curious even if we failed to see as the hidden patterns of the world fell mercilessly into place.

IN THE few spring months between when an electrical fire forced us out of our Queen Anne townhouse but before I took up residence in an office mechanical room for a strange, lonesome summer, I managed to find an abandoned hangar on a tiny airfield—something more along the lines of a civilian country club for aviator nerds than anything significant or commercial—alongside the lake on the north side of downtown. Despite this being the largest, emptiest space we'd yet inhabited, we made a pact that only Denver, Hannah, TC, and I would call this place home (Lily'd been invited to join us, but she was by then already comfortably installed in the Pigeon Queen's closet): after having lost our last two residences (three if you count the university) in such sudden, dramatic ways, we wanted to preserve our new home as long as possible. For a few months, nearly no one knew where we lived, and only on rare occasions did we have guests, mostly Otto and Lily and sometimes Marlene. Through secrecy, we believed we could make our compound last.

Which, obviously, didn't happen. We managed to pirate electricity (a feat Denver executed by means that completely escape me) and so had light to work and live by, but since we had to black out all the windows to ensure no passing random would spot us glowing at night, the space felt monumentally oppressive. Also, we didn't have water beyond what little we could gather in a rain barrel outside, so we either had to bathe in the lake (which, honestly, was kinda exhilarating) or at the nearest Y (less exhilarating, despite what any of the Village People might claim). And too, it was remote: the only personal landmarks it was really close to were the toasted graveyard of our former university and, just past that, the Oral School (which already was getting a little too hip due to those who think proximity to violence is cool). It was probably this isolation more than anything else that foiled our plan for permanency. Over a course of weeks following the brief honeymoon of living someplace new, we each steadily spent less and less time in our hangar, crashing with friends or at least finding excuses to stay out all night until finally, we all jumped ship. TC and Hannah took to dividing their time between the Pigeon Queen's house and the city's Citizens Art Center, where they each had been awarded personal studio spaces (conveniently outfitted with old but inviting couches) in return for teaching a few intermediate workshops each week. Perhaps disinclined to experience more episodes than necessary of The Degradator, I found a mechanical room at the top of a half-vacant Romanesque Revival office building where no one had yet realized the rear service entrance never locked.

Denver, however, loved the hangar. While obviously none of the small airplanes remained, there were tons of amputated parts and banged-up piece of fuselage in the back section of the building and scattered in the *de facto* dumping ground in the weeds out back. A bunch of torches and other welding equipment had likewise been left behind, so where TC and Hannah and I saw a vaulting sarcophagus, Denver saw a windfall. Almost immediately, the hangar became his studio. The tools and materials at hand were all he needed to become again what in his own mind he had lost. After a year of forced exile, Denver could once again bend metal into art.

IT WAS the Pigeon Queen's attic where Hannah and I would hide when it was time for us to get high. I'm not sure anyone else knew how to get up there: the doorway to the narrow spiral stairs was in the back of the closet where the rank rubber gas mask so menacingly dangled, a sort of hideaway door even we wouldn't have been able to find if it hadn't been Hannah's business to hunt out the hiding spots we desired though did not necessarily need.

Even before she on-and-off lived there, Hannah had sniffed out the perfection of the attic. Interrupted only by rising chimney stacks and the few stashed and forgotten things, the attic stretched across the footprint of the house as a single continuous space. Like our eventual warehouse. Like the hangar we abandoned to Denver. There was that haunted-ass wicker crib in the loft high up by the roof's peak, and a couple little storage boxes and—impossibly—an emerald-paisley Chesterfield sofa (which I guess someone must have one time pull-wheeled through one of the attic dormers, though to what end, I can't begin to know), but given the narrowness of the lone and twisting stair, nearly nothing else had been stashed there. Which, for us, was perfect. As time went on, Hannah and I gradually sneaked up a record player and some LPs and Christmas lights and a ton of pillows and cushions and blankets (all of which we gleaned from the Pigeon Queen's hoard), but by and large, we kept the space empty and clear. We could sit on the Chesterfield or sprawl on the pillow pile and smoke dope while listening to Chavela Vargas or Mercedes Sosa, then later use the rest of the room to practice slow dancing or compete in stoner gymnastics, give each other airplane rides, whatever.

In all the years we knew each other and lived together, this was the most playful we ever were, publicly or alone. This room was the only place where either of us ever got silly. We fucking giggled. And that silly-ass giggling was ours. I wonder, though, if either of us ever realized that what we'd sought out and maintained was a secret studio for dance and movement. Whereas TC and Denver faked karate in the mud and locked one another in a fridge, Hannah and I would compete to see who could stand on one leg the longest (Hannah) or complete the most successive/clumsy pirouettes (me) or how long we could successfully share a hula-hoop (a metric as stupid as it is impossible to measure). We taught ourselves headstands and how to somersault into a casual standing position. We taught ourselves to foxtrot. Between our two outward personae, where else would we have opportunity to work out these—our—variations in clownish acrobatics? Where else could we just act like kids?

Were we even aware we were hiding it from everyone else?

SOONER OR LATER I'm going to have to admit that it wasn't just lifestyle choices that changed after my pneumoniac season on TC's couch. The deep cold I experienced in the warehouse had a couple irreversible effects. Like the chronic marrow-deep ache in my feet and shoulders and hands. Like the fact that I'm all but deaf now in my right ear. Because my pulmonary illness went untreated so long, my lungs are forever weak, which means I am forever weak, too, and though like an idiot I still smoke from time to time, I feel the impact of every puff and drag.

So I'm half-deaf now and I guess arthritic and kinda withered because I can't breathe enough to really exercise, my little tits even littler and all my ribs plainly outlined beneath my pallid skin. But also, too—and I have no idea why this would be an effect of extended hypothermia—but sometimes my vision becomes perceptually locked. Like when you're looking at a Magic Eye image and first your eyes cross a little and things get blurred, then the hidden boat or pig or whatever snaps into focus while the whole rest of the world remains out of phase. It happens to me all the time now, when I'm looking at plaid shirts or intersecting shadows or the striating patterns of stains repeating throughout my single bolt of calico. What's near becomes far while flat things become topographies. Nothing I can do will make it go away until some kind of shocker happens, like my body takes a vertiginous dive and I collapse dizzy as fuck to the floor.

All of which means there's a lot of shit I can no longer do and a whole lot more I can only do slowly. Which is how TC got me a pension. He took me to his doctor and made sure every relevant detail of my spanking-new infirmity was noted in writing. Then he did the legwork necessary to get me on permanent disability.

So that's a thing that happened simultaneous to my nesting on his couch, to Marlene and TC documenting his phthalo blue planes, to our long recovery walks in the brownfields where I used to live. Doctor visits and lawyer visits and hearings regarding my reduction of capabilities. For three years I had ceased to exist in any record, had effectively disappeared as our university and all its records went up in mortar fire and flame. All that's over now. For my own sake, TC made it happen. Then he absconded on a one-way train to LA to bury a sister I'm not entirely convinced ever really existed.

WHILE MICROPLANING a slim ribbon of rubber from the edge of a thick black mat, I think to myself how lucky I am to have, among such an abundance of needles and blades and glass, not hurt myself more in my devoted yet amateur practice of construction. So of course, it's right then I slip and glide the razor through the soft meat of my left thumb. (When you're born left-handed but forced to use your right hand for all things manual, you essentially become no-handed in all ways that count.) So now there is blood and it's blood without end. And all I have to stanch the bleeding here in my warehouse is the fabric I've gleaned, fabric predestined for a specific purpose greater than my opened thumb. All that muslin and all that scrim. I cannot get my blood upon them. So I make a different sacrifice. I bind my thumb in the unhemmed corner of my favorite calico, the singular bolt for which I have no other use than to keep my insides in. I add my stain to its gritty and continuous Rorschach of stains.

EVEN BEFORE the police came down like a hammer to evict us from our buttercream Craftsman, I was hunting around for our next free home. It just struck me as obvious that something as nice as an abandoned house in a safe neighborhood couldn't possibly last long: if it wasn't the cops coming after us, it'd be a gang of kids tougher than us who wanted what we had, or—even likelier—one Partisan group or another would set up shop in our area and all illusions of safety would be immediately, violently dispelled. And too, I liked snooping around for orphaned things. It was intuitive, whatever that magnetism was. It also made me feel useful in the hours between getting high and getting fucked.

Since we were already ensconced in a southern neighborhood, I figured it'd be best if I took to seeking someplace farther afield for our next communal home. Where we eventually ended up was a place surprisingly close to the city center, a brick-and-terra-cotta Queen Anne townhouse where I guess the last owner died and the inheritors had opted in response to do absolutely nothing. For one whole fall and winter, we had lights and water and some small degree of heat and, more importantly, plenty of room to roll around and build monuments of trash and throw parties that inevitably ended in some fine new instance of fornication and all in all make general nuisances of ourselves. But none of that had happened yet. I first had to find us a new home.

The afternoon I'm thinking of, though, I was on a house-hunting venture that had me wandering deeper into the rat hatchery of the city's industrial riverside wastes where, after several increasingly fruitless hours, I discovered on a muddy peninsula what I thought might very well be our new long-term squat.

Past a row of warehouses full of bale-eyed rodents constructing metropolises out of packing excelsior and corrugated scraps, out where the blacktop gave way to crumbling shit and all structures declined into torched cellar holes and vacant brownfields (some of which were cordoned off behind the shambles of chain-link fences while others were left unprotected in an open invitation for the gradual accretion of junk and mattresses and trashed automobiles), and beyond even that—where the mucky fill leached through the retaining-wall rocks to dissolve as grey-green sludge into the river—there stood a haunted-ass structure of gables and glass and, most important of all, an electrical line arcing pole to pole from the last warehouse to a meter box on the house's near corner behind a rambling hedge of dead roses.

A more perfect home I could never have dreamed up. This was some straight Shirley Jackson shit. Can you imagine the creep-ass splendor of bivouacking with all your friends within the fallen estate of *We Have Always Lived in the Castle*? Can you honestly picture that opportunity manifest before your living eyes while you somehow *don't* totally lose your cool? With the ungainly nongrace of a puppy giving chase to its favorite ball, I all but ran the road's buckled remains to the house along the water—I remember, an oil tanker sluiced through the river, backdropping the mansion like a Rust Belt Gothic shadow of foreboding—and mounted the porch's swaybacked steps two at a time. A fiasco of scrollwork and glass: the unlocked front door swung open at my touch. I burst inside like the goddamn Kool-Aid Man—all passion, all exuberance—and though the furnitured foyer and central hall smelled of books and food, I raced straight ahead, passing open doorways left and right for the room at the hallway's end. I'm sure you see where this is heading. I nearly tripped over my skidding heels like a cartoon buffoon when I found, there among the sticky tile and greasy stove and piles of unwashed pots and pans indicative of a neglected yet well-used kitchen, a gorgeous tower of a woman wearing the nastiest, most shamelessly stained silk nightdress, pouring herself some tea from a cracked china pot into a cracked china cup. She flashed me a crooked smile like she'd been expecting me all along—not necessarily looking forward to seeing me yet not so put out as to turn me away—then offered me a cup of oolong. The Universe reveals itself as an ordered weave. Then it reveals itself as chaos. I suppose I should have apologized and meekly backed out the door. But I've found that knees have a talent for going weak in the moment when a dream gets crushed. I flopped onto the mouse-chewed cushion of a creaky rococo chair, dropped my head onto the eighteenth-century oak dining table, and in the nauseating throes of sudden defeat, accepted her fucking tea.

And that was how the Pigeon Queen became a fixture in our lives.

———————

WHICH IS to say: It was my fault.

ABOUT TWO years ago—long after TC had left for LA and I'd finally gotten used to a life of half-deaf solitude—I took my first real trip outside this city I've always considered home, on a train bound west into the middle of the world (which is to say, three hours into the unfolding plains) where it turns out the towns are small enough to each be unique. I hadn't anticipated that. All my life, the city had coached me to expect the whole rural rest-of-it to be uniformly boring, each anywhere equally everywhere because there wasn't enough going on there for any of it to be interesting, let alone distinct. But it turns out I was looking at things backward. Because the city, containing everything at all times in every permutation, as a consequence becomes the universe, by definition is everywhere and everything. But a small town can't contain all that. A small town has just a little bit in a particular combination. A granary and a lot of contra dancing. A borderline of wind turbines and a summertime festival for corn. A factory on one side of a river and a small but thriving Vietnamese community on the other. It's like Otto and his polygons. Even if you're limited to only three shapes with which to make a design, there are an infinite number of shapes to choose from, to arrange into infinite new tangents and intersections. All shapes all at once, though, just make for a muddy dot. Which maybe explains the totality of the universe better than any analogy of singularities or expanding, limitless clouds. A pointlessly large city. A clotted, muddy dot.

That, however, has absolutely nothing to do with my trip to see Denver. That's just incidental discovery. It'd been nearly three years since Denver left the city, and in a rare convergence of beneficial whathaveyou, I was living at an actual address when Denver found it was time to send me a letter, and (even better fortune) I was in a position where I could afford to buy a ticket and see my friend. It was early May and since all but essential air travel had been banned some years before, rail transport was cheap again and surprisingly reliable. I wrote to Denver to say I was coming, and a week later I arrived—mildly shocked by the witnessing of our country—in the resuscitating mill town where Denver now lived.

And while I should have seen it coming, I was still a little taken aback that Denver didn't meet me at the little platform acting as the town's *ad hoc* train station: I had to hunt down the building where he lived on the corner of Main Street and whatever, a Federalist brick block the color of a dirty blackboard overlooking downtown with an antique clock store at street level and a hodgepodge of apartments and offices above. The stairway up to his flat was echo-y and cool and deeply noir like something from the 1920s, you know, the sort of place a lawyer or private detective ought to have an office. For no definite reason, the smell and feel reminded me of my parents and their divorce. And despite having stood me up at the station, Denver was waiting for me in his apartment's open door, leaning against the frame with a cigarette limply hanging from his mouth: he hadn't forgotten I was coming or what time my train arrived, he just didn't want to go outside. He gave me a strangely gentle but warm (and also probably our first and only) embrace and complimented my new black suit (some kind of child-sized conductor's getup—not for a train, I mean, but for

an orchestra—I'd found in the boys' section at a church basement swap shop). Then he invited me inside.

I should probably say now that something desperately wrong
had at some point happened with Denver (and I don't mean that
shit with the yo-yo and his dad). His last weeks in the city had
seemed manic and deranged—his nose-first zip through the
world, the tails of his dishwater-grey trench coat snapping in his
wake, had become less an overt yet sincere homage to Groucho
Marx and more the anxious scurry of a playground flasher—and
then, like a single firework bursting in the night, he was gone.
Maybe to other folks it was clear, but from my vantage it was not
apparent at all whether he'd gotten himself into some sort of
trouble, if his own mental equilibrium had finally spun gaspingly
out of balance, or if some other force in combination with all the
above had at last succeeded in chasing him out from his own life.
And really, who can say his shambling freak-out wasn't the cumu-
lative result of decades of buried neuroses? The last time I can
really recall Denver actually *being* Denver was that time at the
Pigeon Queen's house while I watched from the kitchen window,
Denver in a kneel in the polluted muck and tossing the Pigeon
Queen's family china out over the river so she could rifle generations of dishes to silvery porcelain dust, Marlene in her glamour
photographing every blast and toss. They had danced their secret
slow dance while all of us watched and Agustín Lara crooned
what might very well have been an augury, in the morning shot
apart all the dishes, then—what? days? weeks?—later, first one
then the other was gone with a whole lot of breakdown in
between and a blackened cellar hole steaming where the Pigeon

Queen's house used to lean. But the details of all that were pretty murky and didn't seem likely to become much clearer. Denver's letter to me, as far as I know, was the first any one of us had heard from him (though I suspect he and TC somehow remained in touch). So I was eager to see my old friend, as well as a little nervous. But finding him now in this small mill-town apartment was like meeting his doppelganger or maybe his Mormon twin. He was Mister Rogers polite. His apartment was just as littered now as ever with open sketchpads and notebooks and half-made wax forms that (one would assume) would eventuate into bronze or black iron. But there was a certain emptiness to it. Like a stage set re-creating the actual thing. The evidence of work without the work itself. A part of me wondered if he'd pulled all this memorabilia out for my benefit, a little self-conscious bit of theater to convince me he was still an artist even if the work itself had flared to an end just the same as his life in the city.

It would not be long before I came to learn just how wrong my assessment of Denver actually was. But still: the emptiness I registered was real. And honestly, I wonder now if all that was really missing was the dirt. The fingerprints and grime indicative of a life lived and still living. Despite the artsy mess, Denver's new world was spotless.

What happened next was, we sat by the tall open windows of his studio apartment and drank no-name instant coffee. Alongside our chipped yard sale mugs, Denver had set out a bottle of bonded whiskey, but it became clear pretty quickly he had no intention of drinking, so after taking my first sour shot, I stuck to coffee too. I remember, he had on a white T and green duck pants, which made me wonder if—as when he dressed like a business clone to blend in with all the other douchey business clones that'd taken over the Oral School—he was trying to disguise himself among his new blue-collar neighbors. He seemed very cozy sprawled in full collapse across the arms of his leather Art Deco swivel chair. He played around with and mouthed his cigarette the whole time but didn't light it. Nor did I offer him a match. As always, it was the lines around his eyes more than his mouth that did all the smiling. I'm not sure I'd ever before understood just how much I missed that about him. We sat in the warm fresh air nuzzling cat-like through the window and drank our ersatz sludge and looked out over the little downtown—the bank and the consignment store and the bakery across the way, the offices above and few cars passing below, the twin smoke stacks from the factory on the other side of the town's slow river—and from what I can recall, barely said a word to one another. I probably tried to catch him up, the people we knew and whatever had happened to them. But I usually wait to be asked before telling anyone much of anything. So it's completely within reason that I didn't tell him shit. And either way, throughout the visit, Denver smiled and made more coffee and didn't smoke. Like an actor who knew the mannerisms of his role down pat but had forgotten every last one of his lines.

Around four o'clock Denver and I witnessed the bakery closing down for the day and the proprietress—tall and brunette and ringlet'd—walking out the door and across the street with a large white bag held upright in her hands, and a moment later there she was in Denver's room among us. He'd watched her impassively from his window as he had every other thing passing outside. And now, equally impassive, he accepted her in his home. She came through the door and stood behind Denver's chair while saying hello, then Spider-Man-kissed him on the lips before producing from her white paper bag three tall coffees and a pile of croissants stuffed with ham and cheese. She clearly knew who I was and that I'd be there, but Denver hadn't once mentioned her. Her name was Beverly. Her hair was a mountain of chestnut curls.

It was while drinking her absolutely real and delicious coffee and eating our pastries that I learned from Beverly that the factory across the river produced trumpets and other brass instruments—how else could I have known?—now that the textile industry had packed up and shipped out overseas, that people had known and apparently loved Denver's sculptural work long before he happened to move here (or anyway, *someone* local had known about his work), and that the town, in twin acts of arts patronage and civic pride, had commissioned Denver to fabricate several brass sculptures commemorating the town's history and economic recovery, even going so far as to grant Denver the right to install his sculptures at the locations of his choosing. That's what the wax forms in his apartment were about: prototypes of the next round of sand casting. There was already one installed, she said, partway hidden inside a hollow tree in the riverside park, and another discreetly tucked away at the *ad hoc* train station, not to mention whatever others Denver had managed to keep secret in his planting around town. (Given that in civic minds the term *sculpture* is often equated to *monument*, I'm sure the town was expecting grand figures of scale placed in prominent locations. Knowing

Denver's history with size—spanning from looming figures of sheet metal and angle iron to creeping miniatures of glommed-together AAA batteries—and history of subversion, I doubt the overtly monumental was ever in the cards.) He was even given access to the factory's metallurgical resources and tools to make up for any lack in his own metal studio's means. The series involved various amalgams of the mechanical workings of trumpets, trombones, and French horns in confluence with the anatomy of the human ear. Denver had mentioned none of this to me. He just eye-smiled benignly while Beverly explained to me his work. Then she and I, apropos to nothing, fell into a discussion about Jay DeFeo's abstracts and the challenge of training your eye to *not* see austere landscapes within their sweeps and textures and what a joy that challenge was. Which in turn led to the more open-ended discussion of the joys and challenges of unlearning anything at all. Breaking a bad habit in lieu of a corrected skill. Seeing a friend as who they are and not as we've imagined them to be. Reconstructing the narrative of ourselves so as to become something other than what we've been, what we've told ourselves we are. Forgotten as he was beside us, Denver grinned through all that too.

Sometime around the spring indigo of nightfall, I left the two of them alone and crossed town in the cooling dark. Before I departed, though, Beverly pulled me in for a surprisingly intimate hug—one hand in my hair and one on my hip—so that her breasts closed in pillowing around my neck, and without really thinking, I tippy-toed to kiss her lightly on the throat. I swear, if I just turned off my brain and let my body be the animal it is, I'd probably find time to make out with everyone. But if Beverly minded my impromptu kiss to the tenderness of her neck, she didn't show it. I mean, I really don't think she minded. Like a goddamn guidance counselor, Denver smiled and shook my hand, but Beverly caught my eye—all the blood in me suddenly, hotly rushing—and told me to come again soon.

That's when I took my second shot of Denver's whiskey. I literally walked back into the apartment from the open doorway to the table by the windows, drank long and straight from the bottle, and as we'd already said our goodbyes, left without another word.

And it was nice, that quick walk through the purpling evening. Cool air on my skin and sudden jolt of whiskey in my veins. What better valediction could I possibly hope from this day? Waiting on the train platform just a few minutes later, amid cricketsong and peepers screaming their desire, I noticed up where one vertical post knit into the rafters some weird folding of metal that looked like unfurling bells and plunging fungal buttons. But really, somehow, what I saw up there was an owl, watching me watch it watching. My rushing blood had settled and cooled. The sculpture was a creep. It's how I knew it really was Denver's. I boarded my train and pissed one thousand times, making the privy stink like a coffee urn, and it was only much later that it occurred to me—as I was nodding off in my seat, forehead suckered to the glass—that strip her of all cleanliness and employment and the washed and trimmed corpus of chestnut hair piled atop her head and really the entire welcome lure of being a well-put-together woman—which is to say, reduce her to the low bottomlands of unapologetic, abject poverty—and Beverly would be a dead ringer for the years-disappeared Pigeon Queen.

FOR CHRIST'S sake, I wonder how deliberate *that* was, claiming this warehouse on the southernmost river's abandoned industrial portage like some kind of Electra reflection of the Pigeon Queen's manse of the northern river's factory dead zone? Can I honestly attest to a single reason why I do what I do? And even if my motives were known to me: What would that change? In what ways would that change possibly be an improvement?

OH HELL, I do remember now. We were on the lakeshore—it was fall and we'd taken the Red Line north from the warehouse to the last stop almost outside the city limits, where the neighborhoods were vastly untouched by violence and still looked and felt like the 1950s—watching the sailboats knifing with the wind overtop the water, and it wasn't Hannah's father who'd abandoned his first family but her mother, her mom had had two or three kids with some stevedore or dockworker in Mayagüez, then for reasons still unknown to Hannah had packed up and left everyone behind—her children, her parents, everyone—only to eventually turn up again in Vieques, where she first found work keeping books for a man who led tourists on midnight kayak trips among the marine alien bioluminescence of the bay, then later married the man and started a family, meaning Hannah and her sister. This news of her older siblings' existence—not to mention the revelation of her mother having a secret past, one that included a number of unaccounted-for years—was fresh for Hannah, something mentioned obliquely in a letter from an uncle who maybe forgot the subject was hush-hush. Which I suspect is exactly why we took the train out to this quiet acre of lakeside: it was as close to her home on Vieques as we were likely to find out here landlocked on the plains so far from any ocean or sea. In her purple windbreaker, mane shivering in the breeze, she looked positively stunned, and as we sat there on the rocks—knees drawn to our chests in feeble protest against October's chill—above the crashing waves the local kids were still brave enough to dive and swim in, watching the pleasure craft bobbing around way out there and going nowhere, it seemed so obvious to me that Hannah was eager to meet these lost kin. Like she was already looking forward to missing them, for the luxury of having new loved ones to miss. I could recognize that in her, and recognize, too, how alien that impulse felt to me. I was still so scrappy in my half-pint butch dykeness I guess, proud of surviving out of dumpsters and bargain bins and winning fights against white-hat bro-dudes and all the while looking dapper as fuck. Which is to say, I was prideful and still dumb enough to take comfort in my pride. The idea of needing someone—of missing someone—was not a vulnerability I could afford to invite or accept in myself. But Hannah was a million miles from all that. She didn't have to hide the yearning she contained. She didn't even want to. I hadn't caught up to her yet.

IN MY industry, I have created a mousehoard of rubber scraps. Some little more than thin rinds and others like manducated chew toys and others still as usable sheets reduced down into smaller, irregular forms. A portion of which I can, in fact, use (when sliced thin, the rubber's a fine bit of gristle to buffer the edges of glass panes leant together), although the majority is just plain trash, rolling underfoot and threatening to tip me over.

How many weeks (not to mention rolled ankles) pass before I remember that all this garbage can be returned to where it was found? How long do I struggle to work, like a child in a messy room, in a space I've neglected to keep tidy? So this, too, becomes a routine amid my ordered days of routine: each afternoon collecting together and carrying away a portion of rubber scrap, crossing the distance between my warehouse and the derelict shoe factory, two five-gallon buckets at a time.

It takes much longer still to realize: Why must I return to the warehouse with my buckets light and empty? Why can't my arrival and departure both wear the badge of pragmatic utility?

I carry back now on my return buckets loaded with cinders.

IT HADN'T yet started snowing when Hannah's travel grant came in just a few weeks later, each new morning alternating instead between hard frosts and biting rain. The day of her flight, we took an early shuttle to the one city airport still in operation (I mean, the other still operated, just not for civilian purposes) but instead of heading inside the terminal, we spiraled up the ramps of the long-term parking garage until we reached the roof, then roosted by the concrete wall edging the very last parking space and commenced to smoking the final measures of Hannah's stash of opium and hashish.

It feels so silly thinking now about some of the dumb things we used to do. Because of the flight ban, there were nearly no cars in the garage and the few that were there were deeply silvered with the cakey sinter dusting between the levels. So clearly there was no one around: anywhere we chose, we'd be concealed. We could have encamped wherever, could have stood tall on the roof and looked out over the runway with brazen impunity, hell, could have even taken the stairs or the elevator, could probably have smoked *in* the elevator, riding up and down while getting recklessly high. But this was our thing: to sneak and to hide. So instead of doing anything reasonable with our time, we playacted subterfuge and smoked all of Hannah's drugs before she boarded the flight that would take her out of my life forever. Except I didn't know that yet. I thought she'd be back in January. I thought everything would continue unchanged.

My guess is that it was all the drugs that made time slippery after that. I remember Hannah telling me to look out for everyone, especially Lily, most especially myself. I remember her saying something about Denver. I remember her talking but the words not reaching my ears. There was liquid in the air, in the space between us, and it was falling. I remember the roar of a plane landing close by, a familiar sound now unfamiliar. I remember appreciating how everything common revealed itself to be strange. Anything could happen now. I remember Hannah wheeling her yellow hard-shell suitcase down the garage's incline, wheels rattling while I watched from a crouch at our hiding spot by the wall, not quite comprehending the why behind her leaving and my remaining behind. I remember her hair and remember her walk. Both bounced. I remember thinking December shouldn't rain.

GREAT BINS brimming over with sneakers and bins awash in unleathered soles and so many empty bins. Why wouldn't one contain peels and curls of the raw materials compartmentalized from one concrete wall to the next? Over days and weeks, an empty bin slowly fills with the vulcanized refuse of my work until at last, in this one way at least, my warehouse studio is clean.

And gradually at the foot of each vertically balanced glass plane, a small mountain of cinders anchors what it surrounds.

HAVING FOUND a workable studio for himself at first seemed like a healthy change for Denver. A lot of the frenzied mania he'd been exhibiting at the buttercream and the Queen Anne began to wane. The work, in fact, seemed to conjure in him an equilibrium that he hadn't shown even in the institutionalized stability of college. Nevermind if he often used the system of chains and pulleys rattling above each hangar bay as some invented extreme-sport ropes course, or devised a means of robbing a machine shop of acetylene and propane: he overall seemed steady and at ease, in himself and in the world. It felt good to see my friend some degree of okay.

And the work he was making was good. He'd always had an acute fascination with the conjunction of artifice and anatomy (I can remember during freshman year Denver showing me the process sketches in the back pages of *Barlowe's Guide to Extraterrestrials*, how he especially geeked over the drawings of giants whose heads were fortified cities and creatures whose physiology seemed more constructed than organic), but these new pieces took up a more disconcerting residence on the liminal terrain between the birthed and the built. Functioning automata whose sole purpose was simply to continue existing, things vibrant with agency and a secret history all their own (the word *golem* comes to mind). Replicated organs gristly exposed as the single-purpose machines they are. I mean, they were all abstractions: the sculptures weren't *of* anything but themselves. Yet this is what they suggested to me. This is what I saw. The machines inside all of us. The lifetimes the things we make will exist beyond our own lives. His new sculptures were gorgeous, and if

I live my whole life never seeing one again, I worry it might still be too soon.

But when winter arrived and it became clear Denver couldn't continue to live in his unheated cathedral until at least March— that he would have to join us in the rental TC and Hannah had secured with their grant monies—that old panic and anxiety began to reveal itself again. He didn't once more totally lose his shit like when he disappeared after confessing to Otto and me the yo-yo double thievery (after all, he could still take the Green Line east to his studio throughout the winter, could still work until the cold forced him home each day), but still: some black and tar-like thing was bubbling in his brain. He was getting violent again with TC and competitive, pretending it was all a game even when one of them ended up bleeding. Again, he was finding ways to disappear. Even as he wild-eyed laughed and made dinner with us or walked with me in the snow or drew exquisite corpses with Lily and Hannah on the living room floor. Even as he began showing and selling work and hung out more and more with the cosmopolitan underground at the Pigeon Queen's dump. Something was metastasizing within him. I saw it happening and wished I was wrong. But I also did nothing to stop it.

———

MAYBE WHAT Hannah was telling me on the roof was that it was time to get out now. That we were no longer safe and maybe never had been, that our city was dangerous and so were our friends. Maybe she was telling me in no uncertain terms that she wouldn't ever be coming back. We were on a roof and we were in a cellar and we were in twin barber chairs, watching the crows come blackly in beneath the shadow of a landing jet. Maybe I was too stoned to hear her. Maybe I just didn't want to.

RAIN-WRESTLING IN the foul slop of the buttercream's front yard, I one time nearly popped off Denver's right arm. The sort of summer storm where the rain and your sweat have the exact same consistency and heat, like a Louisiana bayou disgorging over your head, the white noise of the downpour deafening. Hannah and I had been standing in the open doorway, sharing a Cohiba Black and watching TC and Denver flip and pommel each other in the churning grey muck. Theirs was an antichoreography of slapping and tripping, each kinda laughing breathlessly as if it was all in good fun when to anyone watching it obviously was not. They were working something out, some childish alpha war, and like a parent who can tolerate everything up until the moment she can't tolerate anything, I all at once had had enough. Somehow Denver had caught TC's right foot and thrust it skyward, launching TC off the ground in a quarter revolution to crash ungainly on his back, and I guess acting on some instinctual and preconscious impulse, I found myself marching across the lawn hollering Denver's name. As soon as I stepped off our stoop, I was soaked: I peeled off my shirt and met Denver's grinning eyes. Seeing what was about to happen, Denver rushed me, aiming to drive his palm into my diaphragm and wind me, but I caught his hand and pinwheeled his arm under, redirecting its force to fall in line with my own (which is to say, at a point far behind Denver) and without breaking stride, used our doubled velocity to slam him face-first into the mud. I remember, through the hiss of rain, his captured breath before the smack of him hitting the ground. From there it was an easy twist-and-kneel to bend his wrist back until it nearly touched his nape. I'm pretty sure my one downward knee descended sharply into his kidney. In order to shout *uncle*, he had to take in a mouthful of dirty water and torn-up grass. I pretended not to hear the first few times he shouted. So I guess we all in time take our turn being the asshole. I jacked my weight hard into my pinning hold like punctuation before finally letting him go. There was no more wrestling that day.

Later, though, as we toweled off in the kitchen, I explained how what I did was unfair. The two of them had just been flailing around like a couple of spastic assholes, undeniably hurting one another but without any discipline or technique. I'd studied Aikido, however, since I was a little shit stapling her skirts to make them into pants, and while much of my learning had disappeared to whatever ghost town atrophied memories go, one thing I'd held onto was the concept of *irimi*, of choosing death, how in any given situation you can either circumvent your obstacle or accept and enter into danger. Either way: you choose. Neither path is better than the other. But in my heart, I know: I always choose death.

At least back then I did. I'm not so certain I buy that line anymore. Without a doubt, opting to live as little more than elective bums in a blasted war zone could easily be seen as choosing death. From a certain vantage, choosing art over everything else—anything else—was very much choosing death. Yet by boldly marching toward voluntary oblivion, was I not also choosing a path circumventing different risks? Such as the risk of engaging with normal people in normal ways. The risk of holding down a job. The risk of being a part of society instead of deliberately skulking its fringe. Most of all, the risk of failing at all these things—the failure to self-stabilize, the failure to pass—meaning none of it would any longer *be* a choice, this life of aloneness and homelessness, this always scavenging for every last thing. Meaning: the fringe was all I was ever cut out for, the only place I was ever meant to be. Because choosing death always means the avoidance of a different death. It also means the avoidance of life.

But like I said, I was too young and proud to fathom this multitude of alternatives, to comprehend my world as anything other than binaries. In that moment in our kitchen, all I could think to do was brag about my audacious embrace of destruction, explain *irimi* like it's the One True Way while watching Denver's eyes light up like a convert at revival.

So maybe that's the moment when we all lost Denver. Maybe that's when he recognized the path he was on, the delicious promise of oblivion at its end.

SOMEHOW I made it down from the parking garage roof and landed myself a seat on the Orange Line, which would take me all the way back into the city where at the central transportation hub—like some glittery arcade where everyone had purpose and I was singularly invisible—I caught a train that would take me north of downtown. I don't know if I made my stop or if I nodded off and later came to on the train's inbound return and made my stop that way instead: the station, I remember, seemed all turned around when I stepped off the train, but it could just as likely have been me who was backward right then. I don't know if I knew where I was going or why I was going there. I remember feeling pretty okay about it all.

DESPITE HAVING helped her out what little bit I can since moving in across the hall three or four years back, I by and large only ever hear from my neighbor via a note slid through the mail slot in my door, always the same simple request to tend to Taquito while she's off getting her blood cleaned up. But a few months back (I guess it'd've been summertime still because the building across the street hadn't yet blown up), her note also asked me to join her for breakfast early the next morning. Which was a surprise. But I accepted (even a solitary crab like me now and again appreciates a holiday from the ascetic routine of a poorly boiled egg).

And it's funny, all the times I'd been in her apartment alone—just me and her fluffy orange cat the same color and visual texture as a hunk of fried chicken—I'm not sure I'd ever really *seen* it before. Framed pictures all over the walls. An oversized bookcase loaded with what I took at first to be dull grey and shallow cookie tins. In her combined living room/bedroom (her one real luxury, a custom-made Murphy bed, burned my heart with envy) was a well-worn cottage-style coffee table and a threadbare Tuscan loveseat the color of eucalyptus, the two contrasting styles somehow in their proximity harmonizing (their stained, scraped, and faded twinning, I'd say, overwhelming all other stylistic touchstones), and centered on the coffee table stood a long, tall, narrow box that I'd never before scrutinized but now, all at once, recognized as an 8mm projector—a Keystone K-108, in fact—with its tiger's-eye leather hood buckled into place. There was even a pull-down viewing screen mounted on the wall opposite the vintage Keystone. All this time, I'd seen it there without it ever registering. How come I could see it now? While my neighbor melted butter and browned onions in the kitchen? While Taquito sprawled purring on a windowsill, emerald half-shut eyes taking my doubtful measure?

What my neighbor eventually served me was a plate piled high with eggs scrambled with olives, fresh thyme, and feta overtop a salad of wilted arugula, grapes, and pine nuts, along with buttery halves of English muffin, a glass of orange juice, and what appeared to be a cereal bowl full of rich reddish-black coffee that I had to hold with both hands ritual-like to drink. My neighbor, though, had only a half cup of skim milk and a small bowl of fresh green beans. We sat at a small table nudged alongside a window (the one not occupied by purring Taquito) and while I ate, my neighbor talked. But I couldn't possibly listen. The food was too good, and all she talked about was her nephew, who sounded boring and wonderful and too perfect to be true. And if we're really being honest, my track record of hearing the actual words of conversations is pretty abysmal. So, instead of paying attention, I *hmmm*'d and *uh-huh*'d at the appropriate times and greedily forked breakfast salad into my face.

But I guess, too (as if any excuse can redeem me from being so shitty a listener), I was also distracted by a picture hanging nearby on the thin strip of wall separating the two windows. It was a 6" × 4" framed photograph of a blonde woman and a cowboy (not a real cowboy, more like a disco cowboy) standing outside before a log-and-grass structure like a tiki hut or cabana. The cowboy looked surprised, but the woman was beaming.

She was wearing a pink crop-top and matching hip huggers while two-handed holding (and it took me awhile to discern this, too, given how small it looked in her clutching nest of fingers) a pistol, aiming and perhaps firing at something unseen.

So there's that too. I couldn't stop my mind and eyes from returning to the woman in the picture while I ate my breakfast and failed to listen as my neighbor talked and talked. Because on the one hand the image was so distinctly strange (what in the hell was even going on that someone—presumably my neighbor—would want to take a picture?), but also, more naggingly, it was familiar. I was sure I'd seen this woman before, seen this *picture* of the woman before. But in what context? And in what context would such a scene even remotely make sense? I munched through my English muffin and pondered my photographic *déjà vu* while my neighbor explained to me all the banal perfections of her absentee nephew, as Taquito—transitioning from the windowsill to an end table that'd double as a nightstand when the Murphy bed was turned down—commenced to dipping his orange paw again and again into a Kleenex box, drawing out each tissue until at last the box was empty. Then he fussed with the struggle of crawling inside.

My neighbor cleared the dishes and thanked me for coming—citing not so much my feeding Taquito as simply keeping her cat good company—and as she fetched her purse, I opened my mouth to tell her it was no inconvenience whatsoever but instead, I said Sissy Spacek. To which she laughed and said very good.

3 Women. By Robert Altman. The photo was a still from the film *3 Women.* A young Sissy Spacek in over her head and firing a strange man's gun.

All but Taquito's tail was now enclosed within the tissue box. My neighbor told me to have fun looking around. As if her home was an Easter egg hunt. I sat frozen by the window with a stupid look on my face, holding fast my bowl of coffee between both hands like I might fumble down some vertiginous height should I let go. Then she handed me what she said was her favorite book (which at first glance I took to be a novelization of Godard's *Alphaville*) and left for her appointment with the machine that'd replace her blood with something more pure.

MAYBE IT wasn't the opportunity to build sculpture again that reinstated some calm into Denver. Maybe it wasn't the winter-compelled distance from his studio that lured his frenzy back. Maybe it was us. He was normal when we weren't around. Alone, he could be himself. But with us an audience to his antics, he couldn't help but perform. And the acts that always worked best for Denver were the ones that seduced destruction.

IT WAS Denver himself who told me he'd sooner shear off his thumbs than accept any help from his dad. I remember that now. We were living in the Queen Anne and for some anomalous reason, when TC came home with a check from his father, no one but Denver and I was home. We were playing mancala in the kitchen, using stolen Reese's Pieces as stones (some lacquerhead had brought us as a gift one of those quarter-at-a-time bubble-headed vending machines, something he'd jacked from a mechanic's waiting room complete with its globe filled with slick-shelled delights). Since we were playing with candy and candy is delicious, it was hard to tell which of us was winning when TC came home from luncheoning with his dad, brandishing the check like the torchbearer in Caravaggio's *Seven Works of Mercy* as he announced his plan to squander its generous balance. He seemed a little let down that no one else was around, but Denver and I didn't mind at all. Luck like water flows where there's vacancy. The three of us went out and cashed the check and after a few rounds at the Oral School (where again we failed to find any of our friends), settled in for a celebratory Chinese dinner, nothing fancy at all but more than we otherwise could afford. Scorpion Bowls and egg-drop soup. Deep-fried chicken parts and veggies bathed in brown sauce. The satisfying crunch of something crisp and golden crackling between your teeth. The boys challenged one another to great slurping mouthfuls of spicy mustard and I didn't have to fake my amusement at their suffering faces and weeping eyes. It was nice having a quiet escape from the occasional tedium of elective poverty.

It was only when TC got up to pay the hostess that Denver spoke his self-directed curse, saying how he could never do it, could never accept one penny more from his father, even to immediately blow the cash on his no-good friends. What change had occurred between our last loud communal suck of Scorpion Bowl and TC's beneficent rise from the table? Beside me, Denver stared at or through TC's back like a marksman taking aim—all trace of mustard endorphins stripped from his affect, a glimpse of Hyde revealed peering through the face of Jekyll—perhaps recognizing the impossibility of ever returning this simple favor of greasy eggrolls and fake-crab rangoons, and told me he'd sooner shear off his thumbs.

It seemed like hyperbole at the time. It doesn't seem so overstated anymore.

IT KINDA drives me nuts, though, not knowing the order events fell into next. I took a train from the airport to the central transportation hub, then another train north, but then what? The pieces get jumbled from there. Before or after heading to the Pigeon Queen's house, I walked the familiar paths of my old neighborhood—one of my many old neighborhoods—to the tarmac of the tiny lakeside airstrip. In the rain and the deep December gloom, I couldn't see the hangar until I was nearly on top of it. I couldn't make out any lights burning inside, but that had been the point: the windows had been spray-painted black and covered with cardboard to keep in the secret of us.

Maybe I was naïve enough to expect Denver to be there. Walking through the hangar's magnitude, I was struck by how—more so even than when we first discovered it—the darkness resounded of abandonment. I turned on some lights and looked around, dried myself as best I could with a towel I found draped over a metal frame (the purpose of which was not at all apparent), and while evidence of Denver was everywhere—in the scattered tools and sculptures completed or halfway built, the bare mattress and hotplate and mini-fridge droning in a corner, in the bucket of shit and piss covered with a plywood scrap in the farthest recess—there was nothing *of* Denver there. Which was different from when he'd normally disappear. Those times, it seemed like he was hiding. This time, he was gone. And I couldn't even tell for how long, how much time this space had required to resume its proud mantel of vacuum and abandonment.

I couldn't even remember for sure when I'd last seen my friend.

YESTERDAY IN my walk to the derelict shoe factory with my twin bucketloads of rubber scraps, I passed two kids—not even quite teenagers yet—sharing a blunt while sprawled akimbo on a waterlogged couch parked on the sidewalk outside a forever-stilled widget mill. Their silence was the sound of fair-weather contentment, their scent bottom-shelf tobacco and really lemony weed.

Today along that same vacant mile, I passed a pigeon eating cold chili fries from an overturned Styrofoam container spilled across the cracked, weedy ground. I was happy for the pigeon, for her having found this bounty.

In neither instance did anyone seem surprised to encounter the other, industrious in our own discrete ways here among the refuse and abandon.

ONE NIGHT during the summer we lived in the buttercream, Hannah and I caught a ride downtown to a club where we knew the kid working the door, a fidgety lacquerhead who'd every once in a while come by the house, share with us his stash of party drugs, then tag the shit out of our walls. I doubt walking into it we knew anything about any of the bands playing that night—they all seemed to be working some distinct ratio of subversive punk ferocity and '70s-era arena theatrics—but it was a chance to see something wild and performative for free, something we didn't have much opportunity for in our current gleaner existence (and too, since my bedroom now had SKEET repeated in bubbly black paint on every spare inch of wall, a free show seemed like the least the lacquerhead could provide). I remember, the singer of one act wore a purple velour bodysuit and seemed to be fucking the whole audience with her voice (and doing a great job of it, too, I might add). The front man of another band did some version of kung fu throughout each song while chanting about space elk and white-supremacist spiders. I mean, I don't know, maybe these musicians were famous and everyone else in the audience knew the score in advance, but this all struck me as unique and audacious and such stupid fun. Hannah cleared a space for us on the dance floor shaking her profound ass, and I consider it quite a personal feat that I resisted the urge to muckle hold of those splendid, splendid hams.

Afterward, however, we were stranded far from home after midnight in a city increasingly at war. Because it was last call everywhere, sidewalks all over were filling up with drunks: across the way was some sort of Euro-dance club, and the dolled-up cokeheads over there were bristling against the punk kids on our side of the street. A bottle got tossed and glass exploded on the pavement. Not even slowing, all the taxis breezed on by (as if we could have afforded one anyway). Knowing full well it was not the most intelligently hedged risk, we decided to walk back to our southside squat: we were invigorated by the music, and the night was July-perfect for a walk in the dark. And maybe, too, we were too young yet—had watched our university get firebombed and walked away unscathed—to believe real trouble could actually find us.

Not that the trouble we encountered encapsulated any earnest threat. In fact, more than anything else, it was annoying as fuck, a grating episode skinning the knee of our otherwise flawless night. We were passing down an avenue of imitation Italianate row houses—likely blathering too loudly amid the late hour's quiet about the sensual landscape suggested beneath the purple velour, the karate chops syncopated to the rattling snare, the crowd-surfing kid we saw drop like a mortar onto the crown of his skull, jump to his feet with hair slathered in blood, and lunge gleefully back into the human fray—when we seemingly at once noted from across the street a baby's stroller, unaccompanied, with a streetlamp spotlighting it on the dreary sidewalk stage. Which understandably struck us as curious. Why would someone leave their stroller outside all night on a city sidewalk? Also: Was there a baby inside? These were important questions to us. We crossed the empty street to take a look.

The thing was an old-style rolling bassinet of nylon stretched over a metal frame, the sort of thing that can accordion up for easy storage. There was a blanket and a stuffed ducky inside but no baby that we could see. Still, we leaned in closer to be sure, and that's when we heard a voice above us shouting to leave it be.

From an arched window three stories up, a large woman leaned out to regard us while smoking an obscenely long cigarette. We hadn't noticed her before. Why would we? Stringy yellow hair hung limply across her face.

Admittedly, I might be wrong, but I don't think there is any set protocol for dealing with moments like these. We called up to the woman explaining we were just curious about the seemingly abandoned stroller, had meant no harm, but she yelled that we were fucking liars and thieves out to steal her shit, that she'd call the cops if we didn't fuck off fast. This struck me then as it still does now as a gross overreaction. I shouted for her to calm down, we were leaving already, but Hannah went a little berserk (because she'd been called a liar? because she'd been called a thief?), screaming at the lady about why in the hell would anyone leave a stroller out in the first place, if she was just too lazy to bring her property inside like a responsible adult or if this was a stupid game she liked to play, some trap she set when her cable was out. To all of which the lady just repeated that she'd call the cops, that we were dykes and spics and thieves, et cetera, et cetera. By now a little girl—maybe all of four years old and dressed in vibrant fuchsia jammies—was leaning out the window, too, kneeling on the sill and gripping the pane above so as to get a better view of what was happening below. She, at any rate, seemed to be having fun. Other people up and down the street were beginning to lean out their windows too now, yelling the expected threatening bullshit and reminders of the hour. Cops undoubtedly would be arriving soon. I grabbed Hannah by the waistband of her jeans and got us the hell out of there.

Luckily, we evacuated the scene before anything could really come of it. Hannah gradually calmed and we passed more quietly, more peacefully through the night until just before dawn we arrived at the buttercream, where apparently there'd been a rager while we were gone. Naked bodies were snoozing in the dewy grass. Inside, a dog we'd never seen before—a vizsla with a magic-marker'd Garfield face expertly drawn on her right haunch—padded happily from room to room while on our only table, amid a mess of crushed cigarette soft packs and ashes and empty cans, a perfect pink cake sat untouched and marvelous. We went down to the basement and got high by the furnace, then fell asleep cozied together like kittens on Hannah's mattress.

So really, this was just another day. But after that, walking around anywhere in the city, I'd now and again spot a stroller left unattended on the sidewalk. It in fact happens way more often than you'd think. Or hope. It's a thing I can't help but take note of. But I know better than to go poking around in them anymore. Not every abandoned thing is for me.

DENVER KEEPING almost always a Zippo and a vial of grain alcohol hidden on his person just in case the mood ever struck and he needed to produce a tongue of flame, something to jet forth from his mouth. Denver one time spitting fire and setting the fringe on TC's denim vest ablaze, then using his own new seersucker jacket to whap out the wagging flames. Or one time getting bored at a party—his own party—and not so much jumping as flipping backward like a scuba diver from our Queen Anne townhouse's second-floor window, the hedge below breaking his fall yet leaving him multiply punctured and limping for weeks.

Denver and the Pigeon Queen engaged in some secret slow dance, an old 7-inch of Agustín Lara playing in the Pigeon Queen's parlor as their two bodies moved slowly in a slither, doing a thing we all could see yet communicating something only they could understand.

Denver throwing dishes out over the river, then catching my eyes through the filthy kitchen window.

Denver smiling, more with his eyes than his mouth.

Denver weeping into Otto's lap over a yo-yo he stole then had stolen.

Denver at the Oral School, one minute laughing—gullet-deep laughing—with TC at the bar then the next both of them on the floor, their stools knocked over and their fists at each other's throats.

Denver on TC's shoulders with his long trench coat buttoned all the way down, the two of them together creating a wobbly Tall Man.

Denver's eyes meeting mine, then smiling.

Denver, without warning, gone.

But did he disappear before or after the Pigeon Queen's house burnt to the murky ground?

BEFORE OR after heading to Denver's studio, I walked the long muddy trek along the river to the Pigeon Queen's. I guess I was thinking I could visit with Lily for a while. I'd forgotten she didn't live there anymore, was quietly ensconced already in the suburbs. Which I guess means I'd forgotten, too, about the entire past year. You'd think all that opium would've had me seeing the hidden puzzle of the world falling into place, but I suppose I must have smoked myself clean through to the other side. An interior space where there was no seeing. Where no pieces coalesced into anything resembling a whole. I splashed through the crumbling streets between the deserted factories and shipping depots, completely soaked through and too cold to shiver. I passed the last buildings and entered the brownfields surrounding the Pigeon Queen's derelict estate. It took way too long for me to recognize that her house was gone. The stormlight was dim, so I must have been closing in on December's early dusk. All I could see was a black outline in the ground out of which sooty grey smoke and steam elbowed up to blend into the sky. It was like watching a volcano seething in wait. But was it eruption or dormancy it was banking on? I stood staring at that smoldering black hole for a long time. But once I saw it, I wasn't drawing any closer. A chalice of smoke exultant in the air. I stood there like a votary in awe.

THROWING DISHES over the river. Kneeling, smiling but only with his eyes. That was the last time I saw Denver. I remember that now. In the mournful hour of dawn, the house drained after the previous evening's crush of people, the only sound the Pigeon Queen's .30-.06 blasting her family china to dust. This was the last time I saw either of them. Systematically destroying an inheritance. The morning after their secret slow dance around the swan.

A MAN and woman—Germans whose names I've never known—sitting on a couch in the unlighted mausoleum of their living room, dour with a child sprawled affectless across their laps.

Tom Waits in his shirt sleeves and fedora, seated and slouched against an adobe porch wall with chin to shoulder and whiskey bottle clasped between both hands, both knees, crooning his heartache into the soundstage night while from a distance, a stylish John Lurie approaches along the wide-open and empty backgrounding street.

Gene Hackman in a translucent plastic raincoat, seated on a bench with one hand buried in a white paper bakery bag where maybe there's a coffee cup or maybe there's a microphone.

These are the scenes I recognize adorning my neighbor's apartment walls, stills from *The Seventh Continent* by Michael Haneke, *Down by Law* by Jim Jarmusch, *The Conversation* by Francis Ford Coppola. Rare sparks of familiarity among the innumerable scenes I don't recognize. Two bears—one a cub and the other full-grown—facing away and standing upright upon a northern mountaintop. A wall painted goldenrod yellow, lit from the bottom right corner and dissolving into shadow at the upper left, the only detail distinguishing this from a saturated color field (something I'd expect TC or even Mathias Goeritz to produce) being, in a bare fraction of the composition near the image's singular source of light, the head of a dark-haired woman gazing vaguely across the frame. A grainy shot of a hooded man with filthy teeth and face tattoos like sharp black fangs rolling his eyes and neck in the sooty light of a camp fire.

Across the room, Taquito lifts the ruffled edges to peek beneath his litter of fallen tissues, curious to find what?, and in this building of ordered, identical rooms—this apartment an identical reflection of my own—I stand in stupid thrilled mystified wonder at the inscrutable life of my barely known, barely *seen* nearest neighbor, one door (mere feet!) away from my own. The only person in this building who I to any degree can say I know. A complete and perplexing stranger.

At her kitchen table and dressed in Technicolor red and blue, Shelley Duvall holds a cigarette with a full crooked inch of ash as if pointing to something fantastic above, smiling too sweetly for everything that's about to go down for her and her family in Stanley Kubrick's *The Shining*. The cat is under the tissues now. The light is changing in the room. And almost, I can hear her delivering her lines. *We're all gonna have a real good time.*

THE PIGEON Queen's attic was always a handy escape for us, but most especially, Hannah and I would disappear up there whenever a party was on. It was almost as though the two of us had some unspoken understanding, we each needing a period of solo (or anyway, duo) calm and privacy to blow out all our endorphins and anxiety in the safety of one another. I remember one time while a billion people got weird downstairs, Hannah and I were playing one of the countless dozens of Agustín Lara records we were perpetually, secretly cycling in and out from the Pigeon Queen's collection—this one in particular, I remember, had something to do with masters or maestros or something—while testing out a new version of airplane we'd invented where, instead of flying belly-to-feet we'd fly butt-to-feet, kinda sit on the other's heels while holding a balancing pose. Which really was more of a trapeze thing than an airplane, but whatever, it was really fun and it gave me an excuse to touch Hannah's heartbreaking ass, even if it was only with my feet. It was such a strange moment for me there on the floor with my legs lifted like jacks to balance my friend above me, to so clearly recognize how attracted I was to Hannah and recognize, too, how strongly I loved her, like platonically loved her. I would donate a kidney or stab a tweaker in the eye to keep her unscarred and alive. I mean, obviously Hannah was the last of us to need protection of any kind, but still: I would do whatever it took to keep her safe from harm. Even if it meant squashing down the wriggling toad of my lust and refusing ever to bite her ass. I would defend her even from myself.

So I floated her above the floor as a reverse airplane and then she floated me, and when the record ended and our stomachs cramped with laughter, we pulled ourselves together and headed downstairs. And that's when, both of us registering that particular brand of too-high surprise, we heard our secret Mexican lover—the voice of Agustín Lara—calling to us from the Pigeon Queen's parlor. And that's when we found at the center of a room crowded with people Denver and the Pigeon Queen slow dancing to "Noche de Ronda" in a slow orbit around her ungainly wooden swan, communicating one thing with their bodies for all of us to see while together sharing some kind of secret we could witness but not understand. She in her housedress and he in his trench coat. Both of them barefoot on the grimed and sticky floor. Slowly rocking to "Noche de Ronda."

It was the first anyone had seen Denver in a month. How could I know he soon would disappear for real? For a missing person, he looked good in the tainted light.

TURNS OUT, my neighbor's favorite book isn't a novelization of Jean-Luc Godard's *Alphaville* but an actual novel, written by a man named Steve Erickson (never heard of him) called *Zeroville* (so you can see my understandable mistake) about a man named Vikar with an unlikely skull tattoo and a Kaspar Hauser understanding of cinema. But what the book more than anything illustrates (at least to me, anyway) is that the problem with film—or anyway, the conundrum, the burden—is the same as that with memory: it only makes sense when organized a certain way. Within the framework of Vikar's comprehension,

> *The scenes of a movie can be shot out of sequence not because it's more convenient, but because all the scenes of a movie are really happening at the same time. No scene really leads to the next, all scenes lead to each other.*

What I think Vikar's digging at is something philosophical and maybe metaphysical. But there's an empirical fact at play here too: a movie is—all its scenes are—a single miles'-long strip of celluloid (at least once upon a time that's how one existed and how they exist still for Vikar and my neighbor and I guess for me too). And just as the entire universe of a film is contained within a single ribbon spooled upon a reel, our memory is contained in the solo organ of our compressed and folded brain. Its totality is simultaneous within its singularity. All time is in all memory, all memory in all time.

AND NOW that I have a chance to think about it—to consider how little Denver spoke in his room above the mill town and factory stacks, how little he betrayed of himself even when we lived together, when we were young and wild and kin—I wonder if he even wrote the letter that originally drew me—if only for a moment—into the calmly eddying circle of his new life. Because why would he? To what benefit or end? The hours we spent in his studio were hours spent waiting for Beverly to arrive. I just didn't know it yet. And Denver wasn't telling. Because it was Beverly's idea all along to make contact. It was Beverly who wanted a visit.

It's very likely she wrote the letter that drew me in.

I REMEMBER in her kitchen on the day we first met, the Pigeon Queen asked me why I was there.

I'm looking for a new home, for me and for my friends, is what I said.

Like the ASPCA looking to place strays, she said.

I am trying to place some strays, yes.

The Pigeon Queen told me we were more than welcome to stay, and I told her we were all set. That wasn't our sort of thing, to live somewhere somebody already lived. I thanked her and told her no.

The Pigeon Queen shrugged and said nevertheless, we should stay. But somehow I knew the subject had changed. She poured me more tea and I didn't turn it down. The world flashes a million signals and gives us a million excuses not to see the signals. It's likely I like the sort of trouble I find. The Pigeon Queen produced a pipe and convinced me not to leave.

OR ANYWAY, film and memory each only make a *certain* sense when organized a certain way. Knowing that Denver was gone from his hangar before knowing the Pigeon Queen's manse had burned tells a different story—operates under and suggests a separate logic and potential motive—than if those facts are sequenced in reverse. In the same way that each of the countless different renegade edits of Carl Theodor Dreyer's *The Passion of Joan of Arc*, variously censored and cobbled together by different hands using different takes and prints, tells a story distinct from the others and wholly inferior to the edit Dreyer intended, constructed, and lost.

So what's the value of a still taken from a film? One single excised frame framed and displayed on a wall?

What's the value of a memory remembered outside the context of all other memory?

How honest are these slivers splintered off from the entirety? How reliable the fragmentary proof? And where in all of this is there hope of finding anything like a capital-T Truth?

In my neighbor's museum of shaved seconds and a single fluffy cat in a box. In my apartment with her novel about Vikar. In my self-executed cathedral of muslin and glass, rubber and shadow, I ask myself and ask again. What's the value of the whole if you cannot remember every part you forgot and didn't know enough to cherish, let alone understand: all the edits fallen underfoot across the cutting room floor?

I'M NOT sure how I made it at last to the Oral School or why there is where I'd go. Habit perhaps. In a confused and confusing matter of hours, I witnessed the evidence of the Pigeon Queen's house razed to cinders and the evidence of Denver's desertion, all while having rode in trains and rode on buses and sloshed through industrial mud yet after having a smoky goodbye with my best friend in the rain without knowing she was telling me goodbye. And then: the Oral School, my body wedged like a shivering goblin against the bar beside TC. I was soaked and pale and finally coming down and TC bought me some dinner—a steak and Guinness pie, I remember—and a coffee heavily dosed with Tullamore D.E.W., then took me to his studio and helped me dry off, let me sleep wrapped naked in blankets on his couch while my clothes drip-dried among his panels of phthalo blue that were almost complete, were nearing their perfection.

How much of a difference would it have made had I just stayed on TC's couch? If I hadn't ever returned the next December morning to my life of denial within the four walls of my once and future warehouse? Did I need those solo six weeks to realize the world demanded I move on? Or did I have to lose my balance and one ear and the full strength of my lungs to make it as far as I've come?

When I told him at the Oral School that they were gone, that Denver was missing again and this time maybe for good, that the Pigeon Queen's house had burnt and Hannah was on a plane for Vieques, TC said he knew. Said it like it was old news. And maybe it was. While TC was capable of seeing the gradual dwindling away of those around us, maybe I functioned still on an infant's binary of HERENESS and GONENESS. This city enfolds us, for sure, along with every little thing we see. All the tiny rivers and empty houses and children torturing small animals in the craters left by Partisan shells. But it also contains our absences. Those lost things are just as easily seen. Just not by me. Not yet. I hadn't put it together yet, the multitudes of presence and absence all my enclosures contained.

DESPITE, HOWEVER, my shameless bellyaching and all the stress I place upon it, I suspect what set the real change in motion—my moment of emergence from pupal dormancy into something like consciousness—came sometime much later, in the year or so after TC left but before Marlene asked for my dubious assistance in administering what very well may have been her final sketchy injection. I'd been wandering the vacancies surrounding the warehouse where Lily and Hannah and I used to live, in my own way taking inventory of everything the last century had found fit to leave behind. Factories of glass and factories of shoes. The mill complex of moldering cotton like a cave-works dripping perpetually from a million tiny leaks in the roof to create a primordial sort of music. None of it ever once varying. No matter how many times I wandered through and wandered again, ticking off the days toward—what? I had no end in sight—further solitude. Not one thing ever changed. Least of all me.

This must have been the end of September, the afternoon air somehow both warm and cool but neither enough to make you say this day is warm, this day is cool. All you could say was this day is late September and everyone would know what you meant. If there happened to be anyone around, of course, to confirm or disconfirm the weather. I only mention this because, instead of ending my circuit as usual inside the warehouse—spread-eagle on the floor's deep scorch, gazing blankly at the burn above, my vision shifting in and out of phase—I climbed the network of open steel stairways and catwalks to exit onto the roof. In the specificity of light and specificity of air, I didn't want to be inside right then. Not yet. I sat myself on the roof's edge where I had a commanding view of my whole empty empire—the forgotten depots and machine shops and foundries and mills, everything jettisoned on the backwash of time for me and the seagulls and the rats—while the glimmering engine of our city's southernmost river, full of all the gathered creeks and rivulets and streams X'ing beneath and between our streets, drained its haggard self at last into the lake. Just river and glass and steel and vermin. Not one single other human soul in sight.

Hannah had had the vision and intellect to document the evidence she witnessed within these buildings, in all these spaces and corners and grottoes—their pylons and girders, cement and steel—proving they were alive and living, that the manufactured is just as organic as the grown. In a space not unlike any of those stretching out below me, Denver had found not waste but abundance, a wealth of unused commodity to, in many ways, build further evidence of the proof demonstrated in Hannah's photography: the manufactured is organic, the organic is manufactured. TC's phthalo paintings couldn't exist without the aluminum panels we'd found—that *I* had found—in a factory that, in this instant, I could see from the roof, between me and the river's final mile. I had found all of these places, and in these places my friends had found life. So why was I so blind to it? Why was I too stubborn or stupid to see that same life too?

And maybe that's all it took, just the breaking of routine. To sit on the roof instead of recline on a burn. To ask where is the life rather than insist on there being only absence.

From my vantage I could see the crumbling matrix of access roads that connected all these structures to one another, and as I observed a seagull glide the length of one avenue coursing between industrial buildings, bank a right at an intersection, and continue tracing the line of the cross street, I saw it both for the bird it was and too as the most recent in a backward-running line of limitless travelers—stepside trucks and tractor trailers and workers on foot or bike or on a city bus—following a path laid down with purpose and a purpose that remains unchanged. The needs of a bird and the needs of a floor boss are indeed different, but only in the details. Their abstraction remains the same. Bodies at work. Bodies in need of a way.

The seagull alighted atop a dead-lens'd lamppost and shuffled its wings in tight to its body, then—comfortably settled on the post's arced stem—scanned the vacant street below for any trace of an easy morsel. Though of course, nothing seemed so vacant anymore. Not to me. I didn't need to see the animals that had claimed this place as their home—didn't need to see the dandelions and weedy grass fingering up through cracks in the asphalt, the algae blooms riding barge-like the surface of standing water—to know that they were there. In the same way my friends had seen the potential for art-making. The way the millworkers had seen potential for a livelihood and trade. The way industrialists had seen potential for a portside manufacturing hub. So many bodies had come and gone, each one recognizing the one thing I'd been missing: the opportunity and life brimming over everywhere.

So what was my problem?

Why did I insist this place was a vacancy?

The seagull screamed and swooped down on a thing. Perhaps I was the one—I and I alone—who was vacant.

I climbed down from the roof and headed home to my efficiency studio, did whatever I do in my home space—washed a dish, read a book—and while I can't really say how overtly aware I was of these realizations and their subsonic notes of epiphany rending through me like the too-close song of a great blue whale, I can confirm the next time I wandered again through the warehouses and factories and mills along the southern river, I was no longer accounting for all the things left behind when industry pulled out in the quest for something more bounteous, something more opportune. I was seeing what was around me for what it could be, what these things might *want* to be. The people who'd constructed these catacombs might be gone, but that doesn't mean what they left behind—this rubber and this glass, these endless glittering threads hemming muslin and scrim—are dead and still. Nothing can resist the violence of motion. My friends had all known this. I was finally catching up. Just as a fire is alive, is fed and then grows, so, too, was this place, inhabited only by me and some animals and a whole lot of ghosts. I could be the feeder. I could make something grow.

CONTAINMENT

AS I predicted that day on the hillside, I never did compose one note of music based on Hannah's photographs. Or maybe it's better to say we never composed anything together. Maybe the project in its very inception was doomed. After all, probably one of us should have known something about music composition. One of us should have just said *this is how we'll begin* instead of arguing endlessly about nothing. (Seriously, *which direction do we read this photo?* or *where do we begin to read?* are such nothing questions: the photo is a moment excised from a continuum, every detail happening simultaneously, meaning every translated note of music would therefore happen simultaneously as well, capable of being experienced and parsed from any point in any direction, over any amount of time, just as every scene on a reel of film exists all at once until fed through the sequencing eye of a projector.) Yet somehow I can't help feeling culpable for our project coming to naught. After all, Hannah was building a body of work all the while, shooting and developing and culling photographs from the world, finding life so obviously organic— so overwhelmingly ripe with agency—among the forge and furnace of industry. What did I have to show for all the time I could have but did not produce the work?

Very likely it is my awareness of so much emptiness—the constant and acute reminders that I profoundly miss my friends and the world we together created—that has me thinking of this again, this potential for translation across media and perceptual organs. As in, maybe the leap from an image to a melody—from two dimensions to four—is, as far as I'm concerned, a false rendition. Like Otto's line and dot versus a square and an octagon. Maybe the only thing we got wrong was the ratio between one and the other. Translating incorrectly. Reading in the wrong direction.

Maybe the planar (itself a representation of three-dimensional space projected in two dimensions) becoming a tesseract of sound (the charted movement of time through space) was a task I never intended nor had any interest in completing. Maybe all I've ever wanted was for TIME to become PLACE, for the past to become tangible. Something I can measure. A space I can inhabit.

———

ANOTHER SOUNDSTAGE night. Elizabeth Taylor and George Segal—both drunk—reclining across the front porch steps in Mike Nichols' *Who's Afraid of Virginia Woolf?*. Elizabeth with a book in one hand and gesturing theatrically with the other, head tipped back like some Raphaelesque cherub, while George, in all his Grant Wood earnestness, gazes with a certainty of doom at whatever future lurks beyond the decisive X of where his ankles cross.

Are either of them aware, sitting there so calmly, how dirty this game's going to get?

SHORTLY AFTER TC left, I found a cardboard box of children's art supplies left out on the sidewalk in front of some kind of kindergarten or childcare center. Given the timing, my guess is they were clearing out and replacing last year's spent supplies before the new bevy of enrollees arrived for the fall, bright-eyed and ready to ruin every crayon. Most of the stuff was garbage— chewed-up colored pencils and frayed brushes and junk like that—but there was a single mini-pad of mixed media paper only lightly stained by what looked and smelled like apple juice, as well as a single one-ounce tube of Prussian blue watercolor that hadn't yet been opened. I've never been one for painting— image-making in general has never been a strong suit of mine or even much of an interest—but with one color on hand and the paper trimmed to a postcard's size, the stakes seemed pretty low. So now whenever I have occasion to think of TC—whenever I catch sight of a blistering patina claiming like lichen the face of some metal thing, when I remember him taking the bait and accepting Denver's challenge to swim across the toxic river from the banks behind the Pigeon Queen's house and only getting a few yards out before his gagging retches forced him to either turn back or sink into the septic poison, when I really feel the weight of my lungs or the weight of my gratitude for having a home and modest pension due to being too fucked up to hold down a job—whenever my friend returns to me if only in my mind, I lay down a layer of Prussian blue as uniformly as I can using a razor's edge as my brush. The stains in the paper show through sometimes better than others. If conditions are right, I'll tape the dried painting to the outside of my window and allow the dew or mist or the city's constant fine snowfall of soot to leave its weathering effect. Then, on the painting's reverse, I write out TC's address and send the postcard on its way. When I next hear from him, by letter or by phone, he does not mention these messages I've sent, my attempts at describing time without having to rely on words.

I wish I knew the equivalent mechanism, though, to reach out this way to Hannah, wherever she now might be. Just minimize and dismiss the distance between us, all simply to say hello. I wish I knew of any way at all I could communicate with Denver and have him somehow without proxy speak back.

AND WHAT'S funny is that, of all the places where my friends and I together eked out an existence—the vacant houses and industrial nonresidences and even the Pigeon Queen's palace of collapse—it's this one warehouse I keep returning to, in both memory and the flesh. Maybe it's simply an issue of accessibility, that everyplace else has been reoccupied by the hopeful or razed and replaced or simply burnt to the ground, abandoned again or paved over for more, better parking. Yet when I first returned here after my recovery on TC's couch, everything that made the warehouse my and Hannah and Lily's home had been skater-punked to oblivion, so what mattered most about this space, too, had been redacted. I could enter its interior, but its insides were gone. And still I returned and return.

And you know what else, while all our other everywheres had been raucous and wild with festivity and communion—the venues where we conjured and reveled in our freedom—this warehouse was a quiet place. No fits of ecstatic transport. No mass gatherings to create and get fucked. Just ourselves and our work and the hushed calm we apparently required. The three of us were still sisters, of course, perhaps more so in our silence than ever before. Yet still: ours was a solemn time together, our home a refuge from the world. A dickhead (Denver) might even have dared call this our nunnery.

So maybe that's why I return here, to this cavern so much like a mausoleum where we lived a monastic, increasingly ascetic life. Maybe I return here because this is where I last lived with friends, the last free commune before everyone began to scatter and disappear. Perhaps all on its own, this place is and always has been a memorial to a life I loved but has gone.

WARREN OATES giving the bleary stink-eye to Dennis Wilson and James Taylor, who are giving the stink-eye (sharper, more ably) right back while Laurie Bird—perhaps by direction or perhaps not aware that the scene has begun, reels in motion and celluloid burning—stares away from the camera and away from these men into the gas station petrolscape of Monte Hellman's *Two-Lane Blacktop*. A big dumb struggle among men for the affections of a woman who couldn't care less.

THE LAST time I visited with Otto was all but accidental. I was walking through the lakeside park (this feels like just a few months ago but really, it was fall of last year) amid October's leafy unblossoming—the crispening color and scent and sound—when I spotted him playing chess with a young girl at a bank of built-in stone chessboards backed by a hedge of denuded, red-berried shrubs. She was small and a deep-peach color and she housed him in fewer than ten moves, a fact that apparently gave Otto great joy, to be beaten so thoroughly and by a child no less. I waited until the game was over before intruding on the particular intimacy of their warfare and saying hello, and after introducing me to Iris—who, it turns out, was his goddaughter, a detail that opened an entire new arena of mystery into who the hell this guy, my friend, really was—Otto took my arm and led me down the park's cobbled paths, feet swishing through growing drifts of flame and copper and gold (apparently his goddaughter was on her own). He seemed paler to me in the watery autumn light reflecting off the lake and smaller, too, yet also quietly overflowing with some wealth of good cheer. Again, there's certain evidence here proving how little I knew my friend. He bought us a paper sack of salted roasted chestnuts and taught me how to shuck the crackling skins, releasing the umber hulls from the milk-white meat inside. While we ate, we watched three brown-skinned women playing with the wind off the water, each one holding aloft long banners of some light fabric—maybe silk or maybe parachute cloth—of vibrant orange and yellow and indigo, the banners rising and snapping and furling with the changing contours of the wind. Then we walked back to his tiny apartment and drank clear plum brandy that tasted like the snowy promise of next spring while Otto played his organ, and more so than ever before I was convinced he was playing his ratios, the music of geometries overlapping geometries, which really were just diagrams for different, many-pointed stars (after all, what's a Star of David if not two opposing triangles succeeding at finding a balance?). Listening to Otto play, I could suddenly understand—I mean it really made sense to me, finally—how a circle contains incompletely its equivalent square, the triangle within its hex, the decagon somehow rounding its five-sided diamond. All these shapes were in conversation with one another, abstract as ghosts yet concrete as bolts of muslin sun-bleached and water-stained, panes of glass splintering razors along each edge, rolls of black rubber and beams of dusty light. I drank Otto's plum brandy and reclined dazzled in an overstuffed chair that smelled like the oldest wing in any library while Otto's rheumatic hands and feet worked the mechanisms of his music.

I know it's foolish and Disney-sentimental to grasp hold of and seek meaning (no matter how ineffable) from one's last interaction with a friend. But with so many of the people I've loved having simply disappeared without fanfare or even notice, I feel lucky to have had this final afternoon with Otto, to have had *this* final afternoon. After he finished playing, Otto gave me a book on kabbalistic numerology (which I promptly lost into the gobbling mouth of the world) and only weeks later, on a cleanly snowed December morning, I showed up at his building with bagels and coffee to find the super airing out the apartment.

Apparently, Otto had lain sinking into his mattress for some days before being discovered by a neighbor's incessant Pekinese. And now it was time to clean. The super seemed stooped beneath the burden of this work, as if he could never afford to acknowledge the human weight of maintaining these rooms where so many lives continue or don't. Looking back, I realize I probably should have offered to help. But maybe already, in this traveled hallway with a browbeaten stranger, certain realities already had me repulsed. From the super's demeanor, it seemed like it'd take forever for the smell to go away.

A WORM'S-EYE view through the center of an ovoid spiral stair, an ascending Joseph Cotten warily peering over the banister in Carol Reed's *The Third Man*. The arrogance of an American bolstered by the arrogance of being a manly man's man—a writer of Western adventure novelettes, no less—all at war against being inept and being naïve in a foreign world so much darker and harder and beyond all guile than he could ever have dreamed. And with all that in mind—what the audience should know but Cotten's character never can—it's impossible to tell which he's more afraid of: that which might be stalking as a sinister tail below or what he might find in the dizzying heights above.

YOU WOULD think—given my tendency to wander and explore, to seek comfort among the refuse—that I would have returned to campus after the bombing. To witness the damage done. To account for what of that life could be recovered. But I never did, I never went back to engage the char and the wreckage. Lily had a rental where she was living that year—really, as seniors, pretty much everyone but Hannah (as dictated by her scholarship) and I (as dictated by always being on academic probation) had off-campus housing—so I stayed with her until her semester-long lease was up, during which time we all came to the gradual realization that there would be no senior shows or theses defenses, that our studios and all the work they contained were likely destroyed or anyway, cordoned by the administration for obvious safety concerns, that the university—with nearly every record, transcript, and receipt gobbled up in flames—was throwing in its hand and issuing us all honorary (meaning *meaningless*) degrees as one last gracious (symbolic) act before final dissolution. All of which was fodder enough to sustain everyone's varied degrees of furor, but for my part, it was something of a relief. My studio was little more than an empty cell, just a desk and an auto-shop nudey calendar and a mesh trashcan spilling cigarette butts through its interstices. It's very possible, too, I was flunking out of Philosophy of the Arts, the only remaining classroom credit I needed to graduate. And in all likelihood, had I attended my thesis defense, I would have failed spectacularly (what, after all, would I be defending?). So really, I hadn't much to lose except my illusory identity as a student and all the repercussions that would entail. Which means that while we all reconciled ourselves to this shocking after-math, I was more prepared, perhaps better suited, for adapting to the world to come: I was already looking toward what we'd next become.

Which left what, exactly, on campus for me to witness? What could I possibly hope to recover? The five of us at that juncture were all but inseparable, always raging and working and scheming, so we knew that whatever next would happen would happen to the lot of us. Yet it's possible I was the first to really know that, to know and know, too, that solid plans had to be put in place. With whatever time I had to myself, I was wandering farther afield, seeking out the perfect abandonment that would ultimately become our home. I was not the brightest or most talented or even the most charming in our cadre. But in this one way, I alone could make it happen. And maybe more than anyone else, I believed in the utopia of our collective dream. Maybe, too, more than anyone else, I was ready to leave my past behind.

SIDNEY POITIER astride a table in some tenement kitchen, his posture and expression as much a dance of unfettered joy as it is the epicentral second of a man's final collapse beneath a lifetime of fruitless struggle (maybe if I could remember where in the movie this scene took place, I could know which extreme is embodied in his bent hips and knitted brows). Ruby Dee and Diana Sands stand back and regard him with the apprehension of all women everywhere when in the presence of an unpredictable man. Their posture and their arms. The whites of their staring eyes. Did Dee and Sands even need direction from Daniel Petrie for this scene? Or did they already by their experience and by their gender understand *A Raisin in the Sun* better than anyone else on set?

—————

BUT I remember now. The blanks between the brackets:

- One week at the Queen Anne when the January thaw coincided with endless rain, the ambient chill cutting all the way to my marrow so that I could not stop shaking, couldn't possibly get warm, and with the whole house stinking of ten thousand wet boots and wet socks and pickled feet, in a moment of weakness, I caved. I bused across town and met my father's lawyer and with the check he cut spent a week holed up at hotel near the financial district, only ever leaving my room to stew in the jacuzzi or sauna downstairs, eating room service and wearing nothing other than a plush robe and looking out my twelfth-floor window at the city and lake below where there were no mortar craters and no glacier of fire on the horizon. I slept in a king-size bed all alone for a week until the rains ended and the sidewalks drained their filth into the sewers, then went home to my friends, renewed and dope-eyed and claiming to have shacked up with an Amazon biker chick, her six white chin hairs, her most enormous hands.

- The teen rehab so far out on the city's west side that we were almost in the prairies, where for three weeks I ate vitamin gummies and drank orange juice until my piss was positively florescent and my veins no longer felt like squirming, bristling woolly bears. I was seventeen. I fucked one of the third-shift nurses every single night. From my window, I watched prairie dogs hustling through the grass.

- My grandmother's summerhouse in Lake of the Woods where I learned the bottom depths of boredom every summer for ten years until I told my grandmother she was a rotten bag and my father, laughing, agreed, after which my grandmother—along with a great many other things—ceased to be part of my life.
- The girls' school I attended from ten to eighteen. Every holiday. Every summer. You learn how to construct your world out of the things you have at hand. My dad's place was only a dozen blocks away, my mother's closer to twenty (I never once slept in her house). Nearly 3,000 consecutive days, interrupted just the one time for rehab. There are only 185 schooldays per year.

This feels like a more comprehensive representation of all the places I've lain my head, again and again lain my head. I think this completes the set. It still feels too few, though, too little for one entire life.

YET I wonder if really Poitier is so unpredictable as all that in his mournful/joyous writhe. If any man is ever really unpredictable. Does it matter whether he comes down from the table meek as a lion or pouncing as a lamb? Does it even make a difference?

I ONE time told TC about the night nurse at the rehab, about our carnal twenty-one nights of recovery. He seemed doubtful, though, citing that *every night* was surely an exaggeration. I asked him how so, in what way—did he somehow question my appetite?—and that's when the weird thing happened: TC stuttered. Then he blushed. Somehow I'd flummoxed the rich kid! He mentioned the moon and he mentioned anatomy then something about probability. Then he stammered the word *cunnilingus*. He stammered the word *menstruation*.

This fucking idiot. Our conversation happened *after* my pneumoniac season on his couch.

After he'd time and again helped me bathe and helped me pee. Moments of intimacy I shared with him. A grown-ass man. And yet: this. Both ignorant to and bashful about the realities— the *visceralities*—of the living human female.

I asked him if he had any idea who the fuck I am.

OKAY, SO while we're on the subject of practical questions, here's one followed by a list of smart-ass answers and possibly one honest response:

How does one transport multiple planes of oversized plate glass from one locale to another, all alone and without a vehicle?

- Don't.
- Through magic (alternately, by sorcery).
- Along proper bureaucratic channels.
- Upon the bent backs of the serfdom and proletariat (*see above*).
- Not alone, and with a vehicle.
- Patiently, and with authority.

HOW ABOUT a dozen rolls of two-inch-thick black rubber mat?
How about endless yards of water-stained fabric?
How about the weight of dust?

———

SERIOUSLY, WHAT on earth would make TC think I'd be squeamish about some blood?

What would make him think I know just the one way to fuck?

IN ERICKSON'S novel about Vikar, the lost original of Dreyer's *Joan of Arc* was found in a Norwegian asylum for the insane. Which is true, is historically accurate, though likely not quite as Erickson depicts it. The film really was recovered—rediscovered—in an institutional janitorial closet sometime in the 1980s. And the original is just as sublime and heartbreaking and transcendent as all the mythology insisted. More so, even: to watch the original is to in a small way become both Joan the warrior saint and Joan the teenage girl, unshaken in her divine convictions yet terrified in the face of inexorable fiery death. Which is to say, it is not a film you watch but a nightmare you share, with Dreyer, with Joan, with anyone else staring agog at the screen, standing as the most immediately demonstrable proof that what we dream and what we endeavor to create are not only *not* different but bare no distinction at all.

———

IT'S BECAUSE he wasn't thinking about me at all. He was thinking about himself. Squeamish in the presence of a living woman's menstruation. Equipped with the knowledge of only one way to fuck.

IN THE months since my original invitation, my neighbor (who incidentally has a name, Norma) has continued with predictable regularity to invite me over for a meal, some lavish dinner the night before or a hearty breakfast the morning of her dialysis sojourn. Mashed potatoes and gravy. Apricot compote on crusty brown bread. Sausage and olive stromboli. Roasted banana and melon sherbet. All the things she can no longer eat due to the sodium and potassium and phosphorus so toxically accumulating in her faultless blood.

And with my mouth and belly full and filling, I am listening better now too. It took me all my life to learn, but I'm listening. After my initial survey of stills, I'd come to expect her to be somehow involved in moviemaking, an editor or camera buff or film scholar or something. But it's just a hobby—a gourmet turned cinephile—something into which to focus her passions now that she can no longer indulge in the rich banquet of foods she loves most (apparently living on boiled chicken breast and measured portions of unsalted peppers and onions creates in its wake a fair amount of disposable income to invest in celluloid reels). While I eat her braised *lengua* or gnocchi with vodka sauce, she fills the seemingly limitless gaps in my education regarding the greatest moments in cinema:

- The grace and grandeur of the slow-motion death match between two roosters in Monte Hellman's *Cockfighter* (which I've never seen) superseding the martial choreography of even Akira Kurosawa's finest moment in *Yojimbo* (which I *have* seen), when Toshirô Mifune in a single uncut

shot katanas to death nine men in as many seconds
(216 frames, give or take, barely thirteen-and-a-half feet
of film).

- Compare that to the live chicken shockingly set aflame in
  the opening of Souleymane Cissé's *Yeelen* (which I'd never
  even heard of before), its animal scream of pain unfiltered
  through any notion of dignity: a samurai being castrated by
  a greedy hoard.

- Then compare that to the "educated" chicken forlornly
  pecking at a toy piano while Bruno S.—riding alongside a
  frozen turkey on a chairlift labeled IS THIS REALLY ME!—
  shoots off his own head in Werner Herzog's *Stroszek* (which,
  can you even graduate from art school without seeing this
  child-eyed nocturne of despair?).

As many movies as I've seen in my life, more often than not I
know little to nothing about what Norma is talking about.
I might be able to stump her with Matthew Barney or Maya
Deren references, but otherwise, she's got me beat. I'm not
sure when I last felt so deliriously thrilled in my ignorance.

And just as much as cinematic history, her nephew remains
a steady topic in her pre-dialysis monologues. His enormous
talent. His unstoppable intellect. His increasingly long absence
from her life. She misses him. As far as I can tell, he's the only
family Norma has, or anyway, gives one damn about.

His flirting with politics.

His impeccable sleight of hand.

The last she'd heard, he'd braved some kind of storm at sea.

Yet in all this time, among all her stills framed and displayed, only one evidential instance of this mystical golden boy have I found (hard to miss, really, given it's the only vertically formatted picture among her gallery), what would appear to be a faded school photo from when he was maybe nine or ten years old, complete with slicked-back hair, a razor-sharp part, and nice striped shirt. And like every other picture on Norma's walls, somehow so goddamn familiar.

Too familiar, in fact.

The unwavering calm and control of someone who never once in his life has felt shaken by the world's insistent chaos.

Smiling not so much with his mouth as his eyes.

AND WHILE we're flirting with the subject of conspiracy: since my visit, I've never once replied to the letters Denver sends or Beverly signing as Denver has sent, whichever it might be. I'm sure some of what I feel is simply paranoia. I'm sure in many ways Denver is recovered or in recovery, is just like me and wants to reconnect with the friends he's lost despite his flawed yet earnest love. Something about the arrangement, though, screams that I'm going to lose big. A pie in the face or my cheeks pinned between my knees. Forced into someplace I do not want to be. And I suspect, now more than ever, I've suffered enough degradation for one lifetime.

I **MEAN**, I get it, it's crazy to suggest any cryptic interpretations of my neighbor's nephew's photograph. It's crazy to see the likeness to Denver and his anti-smile smile and think it means a thing. Just as it's crazy to see the resemblance to steady, self-possessed TC and think that means anything either. I know this. But still: the unwavering calm, those fucking eyes. It's aggravating having to wrestle with the fact that the face in the picture's so awfully damn familiar.

So I do my research. Walk the blocks to the nearest branch of the public library (or anyway, the nearest branch not closed due to fire or collapse or conversion into an emergency shelter). Find the reference desk and get pointed in the right (albeit vague) direction. Start pulling every relevant-looking 791.4 book of photos from the stacks.

The search, of course, would be a lot easier if I was starting with a name and searching for a picture instead of the other way around. But in time I do, in fact, find the match I'm looking for. In an anthology comprising several decades of *Vanity Fair*, a themed collection of photographs depicting famous people from when they were young.

The card-sharp eyes.

The raconteur's unconcern.

A charmer before he was anybody.

Robert the fuck Redford.

The photograph on my neighbor's wall is of Robert Redford as a ten-year-old nobody.

My neighbor Norma is insane.

ONCE IN the fall before our collective dream untethered to its ends, I came home to our warehouse from a list-making walkabout to find Hannah and Lily together among the fluttering wings of their wet prints drying along their interweaving cord lines. Ankles crossing and uncrossing left to right. Stepping back, then a quarter-turn. A loose synchrony as they tried not to bump heads. Lily was teaching Hannah the Electric Slide. And watching them dance together among their combined hanging prints, I felt a part of me break that I had not known could be broken.

I wanted to teach Hannah the Electric Slide, you see. Except I didn't know that dance.

In our secret studio above the Pigeon Queen's empire of lack, it was always Hannah who taught clumsy me how to move.

AFTER SHE moved out of our warehouse, Lily and I for a while lost touch. Not because of some falling out or anything like that (it's not her fault, after all, I felt possessive of dancing with Hannah: it's my fault). It was just the uncaring whim of circumstance. I got sick and consequently laid low for really the rest of that year, only ever seeing TC and Otto and now and then Marlene. Lily, for her part, had found a place on the lake's northeast shore in a chill, suburban neighborhood where no violence had yet to come (the very neighborhood where, just months before, Hannah and I had sat on the rocks above the water's edge, watching the brave boys dive and sailboats bob while Hannah told me longingly about the family she never knew she had). Her roommates, from what I gather, were a bunch of sweet young women who worked actual jobs at schools or libraries or whatever. So, you know: there was a lot at play to keep us apart.

But a few years later we crossed paths again, at a basement leather bar called The Bug That Bites. She, of course, was there with her camera, as much a part of the scenery as anything else. And me, well, I get curious. Anyway, in the red lights and very exposed humanity crushing in to the hammering industrial soundtrack, the two of us somehow found one another and truly, it was a surprisingly boisterous reunion. Not even while thrashing in an epileptic fit against my open mouth had Lily shown such excitement (that might be an exaggeration, but still). We spent the next few hours dancing and buying each other drinks and shouting over the music, arms dangled over shoulders like soldiers on the surviving end of a war. The bloody lights on her hair made her look delightfully hellish. I remember, beneath the vodka tang of our drinks, her skin smelled like cherry blossom lotion. But sometime around midnight she abruptly announced she had to head home, she was turning into a pumpkin, and just like that, she was gone, leaving me blitzed and more than a little turned on with both our drinks to finish. I hung around until last call, then later had the chance to discover how a bridle and bit feel and taste. So all in all, it was a pretty good night.

But after that, Lily and I kept in better touch. TC by then was already permanently sunk into the mire of LA, and of course Hannah and Denver and the Pigeon Queen had long become phantoms in the ambiguous, abounding wherever. So it felt especially good to have again my friend. We one time got gussied up (or anyway, Lily got gussied up and I washed and wore my least shitty suit) and took Marlene to a raucous and dykey burlesque and cabaret. Another time, we chanced upon Otto at the Oral School and got our old friend fantastically drunk on Bohemian pilsner and dogwood *rakija*. On the whole, Lily seemed more expressive, more *vital*, than she had before. She spoke more loudly, she commanded more space. She laughed like a giddy child gone wild on sugar and fun. It was as if in those intervening years something had come unlocked within her (perhaps that's what happens when you live in a safe place with safe people). Either way, these few months of reunion proved us closer than we'd ever been. We never fooled around again, of course, or even so much as kissed. We didn't have to.

Then, just as before, Lily again faded out (it's hard not to append an *on me* to that statement). We still saw each other every now and then, and our times together were just as exuberant and audacious as ever. But more and more, it seemed as if she was gradually slipping away. I can imagine a dozen different reasons for Lily wanting or needing some distance from me—I can often overdo it partying and know my recklessness is contagious, when I'm not quiet and withdrawn I'm picking fights with dudes way bigger than me, and yes, my libido is not nearly as under control as it really maybe ought to be—and in every instance, she'd be justified in defining some boundaries. I know this. I get it. Knowing that and feeling the consequences, though, are desperate worlds apart. Months would pass without word from her, and even then it often was just a quick call. Like she was checking in. Making sure I was okay. Then one day after months of silence, she phoned to tell me the details of Marlene's death and funeral. The military cut. The name on the grave. She'd gone alone to Pennsylvania to see our friend into the ground. She shared with me this information as if that's all it was: information. There could not possibly be more distance in her voice. I didn't ask why she hadn't told me sooner or hadn't asked me to come along. Again, I guess I didn't have to.

As if this were a funeral for more than our lost friend, Lily stopped calling after that.

HER FORMICA table was Crayola blue and shaped like a tablet of aspirin. There were deep chips and gouges in its face as if at multiple times throughout the years it'd been struck with a tool and some incarnation of violence. It was only then, seeing those marks, that I began to wonder about the sort of men Marlene allowed into her life and her bed, and with that wonder began to worry, even as I knew my worry was appallingly late. The ceilings were tall so the kitchen cabinets were tall, too, and only a few of them had doors, allowing me to see how empty these spaces were kept or had become. A shelf with a box of cereal and a can of soup. A shelf with a couple plates and a bowl holding what few dull utensils she might need. The electric kettle, though, was a nice Japanese model that sang when it reached temperature, and the whole time we drank our Nescafé and cream—I remember, amid everything else, it was *real* light cream, richer than half-and-half—Marlene kept her sharp chin turned down, her thin wrists crossed in her lap. It's important that I remember this. Her chin was down and her wrists were crossed as steam rose from our Nescafé and for only the second time ever, I was aware of her secret, aware that Marlene could be reduced, made low and made to feel shame. The secret that anything could be taken from her. I couldn't understand why I was meant to see this, why she had chosen me. I hope I can understand now, though. I hope I haven't failed my friend.

A beat-up table and instant coffee steam. The blue of a jaw-line shadow no one was meant to see. And me. Together we completed our composition. Then Marlene took my portrait, and I was gone.

BUT WOULDN'T that make me insane too? Thinking my neighbor's supposed nephew is anyone I could possibly know? What's it say about me that I'd even suspect? Life's obvious patterns I miss and miss again while imagining—pursuing, even!—hidden patterns of conspiracy that make absolutely no sense. Like Beverly looking enough like the Pigeon Queen to maybe somehow *be* the Pigeon Queen. Like anyone other than Denver writing letters signed with his name. My neighbor somehow the aunt of my one or another best friend.

What's this say about me?

STARS. MAYBE all Otto was really digging at was stars. Why he preferred an intersection of square and octagon to a square and a line, a line and a dot. Some ratios could be drawn as stars while others could not. I know it sounds hokey as fuck, like something your corniest maiden aunt might dream up, but really, given the chance, who wouldn't prefer to compose and perform the music of the most perfectly rendered stars?

BUT I was wrong before. Wrong or just overly romantic. Because I have seen Marlene—in fact have *many* times seen Marlene—in the full light of day, long before her last injection and before being made small by a cafeteria busboy. Like the spring morning when she and Denver and I walked the endless network of bridges between the house party we'd crashed and consequently seen the debauched end of and wherever the hell we'd parked Marlene's car. (I know she drove the thing—she had to have sometimes driven her car—but if ever she was accompanied by anyone else, she always sat in the back and made them take the wheel.) Along the way as we searched and wandered those early-hour streets, I had them wait while I sketched a tree whose limbs looked like the exaggerated gestures of an overwrought conductor flailing before his orchestra, its branches erupting in a foam of brilliant pink despite winter's persistent chill, and once I was done, Marlene looked at my sketch then kindly took my pad and pen, drew her own version of the tree, faithfully and expertly, and underneath wrote in declarative block caps REDBUD. Or really any of the times we witnessed an evening release itself to the purple of dawn while we denied our exhaustion was a hangover waiting in the wings. Or all the times she and TC accompanied me in my recovery walks, sur-veying the factories and brownfields while May coaxed some involuntary hope with its light, with the scent of earth reclaim-ing itself from April's pungent muck. The one time we came upon children at play, so clearly skipping school, and Marlene took their pictures—she asked if it was okay and they said sure—not using her chunky studio camera but a small twin-lens

Kinoflex like a traffic light hanging from her neck that nevertheless somehow blended seamlessly into the asymmetric cut of her black wool coat. She took their pictures while they wrestled and ran, her hair glowing—gleaming, really—like coils of polished gold. Marlene unconscious of herself because she was completely within the universe of her viewfinder, the universe of her lens. Marlene laughing with a clutch of wild, unattended children.

Why on earth would I want to forget this? Marlene not only the calm master of her art but its joyful heart as well. Marlene in the forgiving full light of May. Why would I deny this of her in lieu of a romantic fiction?

NORMA, OF course, is not insane. In fact, she's on the right track. Where is the failure of logic in preferring a fantasy over reality's staid banality (isn't this the mental function, after all, that allows us to fall in love)? Why not go one step further and commit wholeheartedly to the illusion, to live within the universe paralleled in the movies? Be Mifune slaying bandits for honor or for pay. Poitier dancing or weeping or both in a hysterical ecstasy atop a kitchen table. The aunt of Robert Redford, who likely lives someplace less austere than in an efficiency apartment in a city at war with itself, who can dine without qualms upon her most loved foods without fear of chemical betrayal coursing through her blood. Who wouldn't choose a life of fantasy? Conceal the daily tedium in the trappings of compelling artifice. Fill your walls with the family album culled from your favorite dreams, manufactured by unmet intimacies, the strangers you've always known.

JUST TO keep the record clear:

I've seen Denver flip backward out of second-story windows, and I've seen him attack people—attack his own best friend—for no reason whatsoever. I've seen him incoherent on a park bench sharing a bottle with a homeless man, and I've seen him shirtless in the rain. But I've also seen him knock a man to the ground for having tried to hurt a kitten. We were walking together in the January dusk while I looked for new trees to draw or maybe the same trees to draw again when first we saw on the opposite sidewalk a tuna-steak grey blur of kitten running for its life, then a black-booted skinhead chasing after, moronic in his attempts to stomp the kitten into the pavement. Denver and I saw this together while standing side by side. Then Denver was across the street and the man was on the ground, the back of his bald skull like a felt pen reddening the sidewalk, a transition in time and space as illogically fast and abrupt as a poorly spliced edit in a film. Denver didn't kick the downed man or bend to hit him again, just loomed like a granite hammer ready to fall while the skinhead first scuttled backward on his ass, then finally turned over, found his feet, and ran like the coward he was and likely still is.

The kitten, of course, was gone.

So I've seen Denver as a feral basket case fit for any sanitarium or county lockup, and I've seen him defend the life of a kitten he did not know and would never see again. And I have also seen TC—our calm and moneyed protector—nudge with his penny-loafer'd toe the bodiless wing of a pigeon off the sidewalk into a muddied street drain without so much as a hitch or pause in the flow of whatever he was saying.

And in all these instances, I never said shit. Not to interfere and not to encourage. Informed by the wrongheaded belief that none of this involved me: I kept my stupid mouth shut.

AND BETWEEN readjusting for the zillionth time the final narrow plate-glass cells and making one last ascent to the rafters above to attach and unfurl long tongues of stained muslin and watermarked scrim, how can I possibly deny the appeal of living within a manufactured dream?

IT WAS months after Otto died that it at last occurred to me: I should have asked his super about the cat, if among Otto's affects he had found, living or dead, a cat. I felt so inept and stupid, too recklessly immature to be treated or trusted as an adult among adults. What the hell would happen to the cat? I imagined the poor creature sneaking out the open apartment door and down the hall while the super, attention elsewhere, cleaned and aired out Otto's place. I imagined the cat slowly starving to death in the company of its master's corpse, impossibly resisting the temptation to eat the vacated flesh of the human it once loved. Then I imagined Otto alive and spending his days in his cramped, dusty set of rooms, his only companion a tuna-steak grey cat more at home hidden behind furniture than anywhere it might be seen. Then I imagined how easy it would have been to visit my friend a little more often, and then I stopped imagining anything after that.

And maybe that right there is the kernel that grows the whole tangled garden of the problem. We have our friends and we have our lovers and are convinced we know who they are. But we're just playing make-believe, taking what evidence we can see and hear and taste to justify what we've imagined, what we've decided in advance must be true. I can sit here at my desk overlooking the street below or in my warehouse among muslin and glass, convinced I'm remembering and missing my friends when really, I'm just inventing imaginary people, over and over again reconstructing the same imaginary people. Imaginary Otto. Imaginary Denver. Imaginary kitty hidden among books.

Did any of them ever really exist?

How would you even know?

Not one of us can really know anyone.

So I begin by wishing I'd asked about the cat and end by wishing I'd thought to ask the super if Otto was really Otto's name. Or anyway, what his last name might have been.

EVERY TIME I go to visit Norma for our predialysis meals, there's a fresh box of Kleenex on the end table beside where the Murphy bed is turned down each evening. Every time, while I eat my ragout and gnocchi and Norma talks Lupino or Varda, Taquito one by one paws out the tissues, crawls into the box's ovoid aperture, and purrs himself to sleep.

After so many repetitions, so many variations on this set and scene, I can't help but wonder how intentional—how known— this whole ritual is. Can't help but wonder, among all our explicit and implicit actions, who in this triad serves whom.

———

I GUESS one list I have continued to keep is the collected names and vitals of women who have disappeared since the bombings began. Of all the changes that have come over the city this past decade of fierce and intermittent violence, this is one change I can stand behind, how the city papers across the board have made it a free service to anyone looking for a lost loved one to share information about who they're looking for. And while men do now and again pop up in these pages, by and large, these are compendiums of women lost.

This isn't information I copy down anywhere or even cut out from the papers to bind or file away, at least not since the warehouse was skater-punked and all my notebooks disappeared. It's a mental list now. I read their names and study their headshots if any are offered, learn as much as I can about who they are, who they might have been. Create for myself a living picture in my mind, to remember as best I can these details, though to what end, I can't say. Without doubt, all of these women and girls are dead, pulverized in the collapse of buildings or suffocated in basement shelters beneath the intractable weight of debris. Or worse. Never will I pass one of these women on the street. Not one. But someone else out there has hope—a parent or a lover or a friend—so I'll hope along with them. Just as they remember, I, too, will do my best to remember.

In all these years, never have I come across a listing posted by either one of my parents. Not once have I read a description of anyone who might just possibly be me.

I **WONDER** if that's something else Marlene could have identified with, never seeing her name listed among the women lost. As if her parents, so far away, couldn't care about the danger that might have swallowed their kid. Or if maybe they only ever posted about a son named Marcus who no longer existed and, in many ways, never had. I wonder if Marlene ever saw those posts for a missing son and ached for the family that didn't know enough to know it was a daughter they'd so long ago lost.

I wonder if the ache was knowing they weren't looking for their missing son either.

YET ULTIMATELY—unbelievably—it's the problem-solving that invites the one real joy and intangible reward for translating memory into form manifest. Not the theoretical solutions marked down on paper (that's how I lost a decade into notebooks that eventuated into the thin ether of the unknowable world, which is to say: fuck all). I mean practical solutions, the utilitarian uses of my body and mind that prove I'm not such a boob after all. Such as:

- One bucket fits neatly into another, allowing a free hand with which to carry a rake to the patch of cinders in the sulfur reek of a cellar hole. But what about after you've raked the cinders into your buckets and must return across the industrial peninsula to your warehouse? Or, worse yet, what if on your journey to the cinder pile, your buckets are full of rubber scraps in need of discreet disposal? In either instance, your previously free hand is bucketed now. <u>Solution</u>: Feed the rake's handle through your vest and across your shoulders yolk-like from one arm hole to the other. You'll absolutely look like an idiot. But there is truly no human here to see or to judge.

- Because the rafters are precisely 36' 6" from the warehouse floor, it does not matter how the fabric is affixed above as no one can see such detail from below (assuming, of course, there will ever be anyone but me to see). Use whatever means is easiest and dependable to create a clean, straight seam to the bubbly spray of retardant coating each beam.

[Tangent: Is a length of fabric 60″ wide descending 438″ to the floor a pleasing ratio (10:73)? Why, yes. Yes, it is.] But what about the bottom end of the unfurled bolt? How do you affix that skirting edge in a way that draws taut the fabric's full length and is also aesthetically pleasing and consistent? Solution: Return to the abandoned textile mill where you originally gleaned your fabrics. Find a bobbin of gold thread that's just as stained and weathered as the fabrics you've hung throughout your vacant space yet still, like your fabrics, retains some luster of its original design. Bend a thick needle into a hook and learn how to sew like you're stitching an open wound. Hem the fabric into the wheel of rolled rubber you've already laid like sod onto the floor. Repeat eighteen times until the alternating bolts of reclaimed muslin and scrim duplicate imperfectly their patterns of water stains and weather and grime from rafter to rubber, their footprint forming an intermittent hexagon through the air.

- How do you all alone stand three panes of plate glass 6′ tall and 3′ wide to balance upright and together as a looming triangular enclosure pointing outward like an arrow's head? Solution: Through patience. Through the acceptance that the resultant geometries are not perfectly equilateral but subtly unique (which is to say, inconsistent) in their angles. Through the knowledge that such inconsistencies are all but invisible and as consequence, effectively don't exist. Through the strategic placement of a thin membrane of sliced rubber between the touching edges of glass so that each holds fast (rather than grinds) against the other. Through the gentle application of raked-up cinders piled at the base of each plane, anchoring each in place on the wheel of black rubber on the floor. Repeat twelve times until the outward points cumulatively plot an intermittent dodecagon through the room.

- How do you render a perfect circle of black rubber 219" in diameter (which is to say, a ratio of (2:1) to the distance between the ceiling and floor)? <u>Solution</u>: Centered over the scorch mark on the floor and below the scorch on the ceiling, roll out a square of black rubber larger than you need. Measure to find its exact center and drive a nail into this focal point. Tie one end of a length of string 109½" long to the protruding nail head. Tie the other end to a red Sharpie. Keeping the string taut, draw a red circle on the rubber. Learn to accept imperfections. Slice away the excess rubber. Learn again to accept imperfection.

- How do you account for the changing light day by day and season by season moving through the warehouse windows? <u>Solution</u>: You don't. Let it account for you.

- How do you account for the fingerprints and smudges on the sheet glass? The untraceable and likely toxic industrial dust settling through the air onto everything like the most crystalline powdering of snow, begging for an arrest of motion that cannot possibly come? The scuffs and tears in the imperfectly cut rubber concealing the scorch mark on the floor? The still-lingering scent of developing chemicals wafting from Hannah and Lily's former darkroom where a rat may or may not be nesting? How all these things together create an obvious way in yet no dependable way out? The evidence indicative of a life lived and still living?

You don't. You don't. You don't.

THIS PAST fall, after a summer of mostly undisturbed peace—the sort that had many folks wondering or wishing that this might signal the end to the increasingly pointless Partisan war—a series of coordinated bombings shook across the city, lakeside to western sprawl. All indications were that some new resistance group had formed: unlike every other militia before, there was no consistency to the targets, no deference given to civilians or to residential neighborhoods. The perpetrators appeared to distinguish between no one. Citing no cause or platform, they ignited their bombs and launched their mortar shells indiscriminately and anonymously.

As it was, it was this meaningless salvo that finally marked the conflict's unresolved end. After three autumn weeks of unpredictable daily attacks, the bombings stopped for good. Which, in its own way, was just as shocking as when they began. The entire city's routine of life seemed on pause for the following month as everyone labored to get our world back in order, reestablishing utilities and phone lines, repairing blasted train tracks, clearing rubble from the streets. During the final barrage of mortar fire, the tenement across from mine took a direct hit to the roof, an explosion that left the structure standing but blew a hole straight through to the subbasement. Which meant there was no longer a central stairway or elevator. While some of the apartments after the blast still had workable fire escapes, over a dozen occupants throughout the building remained stranded with no obvious, safe way down. After determining that there wasn't any fire or leaking gas mains, all of us—everyone in the neighborhood who could help—worked together to get the trapped out as safely as we could. Using a single extension ladder (the only one we could scare up on such short notice) and a whole lot of hope, the nimblest among us (which is to say, me and three teenage boys who'd been stoop-sitting when their building took the hit) ascended through the exploded interior one mangled story at a time, then starting at the top floor ferried down the marooned one by one, at each floor collecting more and more people so by the end we had a crowd of oddly calm, almost-playful rescues pilgriming down our one ladder from the second story to the ground's safety below. For a couple days afterward, I tried my best to help in the cleanup—slinging a shovel or pushing a wheelbarrow—but after being so long inside the blasted building, my weak lungs weren't up for the task. It'd be another week before the fire department came to rescue the already-rescued, and longer still before the city demo'd what was left of the gradually tilting building. Like so much else in the city, all the municipal services by then were stretched impossibly thin or simply no longer existed.

The papers, though, remained in operation throughout, reporting the scope of damage, the (mostly symbolic) destruction of the financial district (which, after all this time somehow avoiding the shelling, was now little more than a blackened empire of I-beams and concrete elevator shafts: a city's skeletons exposed), the eventual and creeping progress toward reconstruction, the neighborhoods that had regained water or power or public transit, the names of those missing or accepted as lost. It's how I learned Lily's neighborhood had been among those most fiercely attacked. How the houses that weren't bombed were consumed in the resultant firestorms sweeping like a lashing tail. How the bridges crossing the rivers and canals were all variously destroyed, trapping nearly everyone on the side of the fire. The papers showed pictures of what was left of the neighborhood, which was all indistinguishable because all of it was black. The papers listed the names of those missing or accepted as lost.

In this one instance, I cannot buy into the illusion of hope. There is no living picture to create. No means of detail to identify those lost. Like an error erased from an accountant's ledger, that neighborhood and everything in it is simply gone. It's how I know Lily's disappeared and isn't ever coming back.

THAT ONE kitten's the only one, the one Denver saved: the only tuna-steak grey cat. No matter how hard or long I look. Nothing has ever come close to the perfection of that one terrified kitten's native design.

BUT I wonder now if it ever really mattered what Otto *meant* with his geometries, if it could possibly make any difference whether his music was scored, improvised, or somewhere in between. In his age and in his solitude, he found he could tell me his ideas about the numbers underlying all things, found he could share his music and share his brandy, and I for my part could listen, could *be* there, attentive and warm in his apartment and cozy in his armchair while watching those fucking bubbles stream so ridiculously from the bowl of his pipe—stem vised between his teeth as he puffed and hummed a melody counter to the one his agile hands played—and keeping my eyes out for any evidence of a hidden cat who may or may not exist.

Why does it have to be anything more than this? Why would I want it to be?

ONE DAY recently while walking out to the cinder patch with my buckets and my rake, I came upon a boy playing on the cracked blacktop outside a derelict shipping depot (the logo painted in faded yellow and blue along the building's concrete side boasted in slanting modernist typeface THE FRUIT SHACK 5, LLC). The boy was maybe five or six and all alone squatting on his haunches or sometimes falling forward on his knees, stacking random bits of detritus—busted pieces of crate and foam packing excelsior and stray bolts and a dented tin lunch pail—into a nonce and purposeless structure. I said hello and he said hello and that about exhausted what we each had of that kind of thing. While the clouds rumbled up darkly above us, I stood for a spell and watched.

I recognized the boy from the cadre of urchins I see running around out here sometimes, have seen running off and on for years. They always look well fed and are no dirtier than any other children at play, so I've never had much cause to worry after them. Every few years I notice the little ones have become the big ones while the big ones've cycled out in pursuit of other, newer, big-kid games. But this little guy, as far as I could recall, was the littlest of the littles. And today he was alone. Stacking garbage in an architecture destined to fall down.

This was a game I'd seen the other boys playing recently, some kind of team competition to see who could build the tallest structure and have it stand the longest. In the way of little kids everywhere, this solo boy understood the game's method without benefit of the concept. His structure rose in terraces that terminated unexpectedly and way too low, pointless annexes peeling off in either direction, a twisted Sterno can (which, where even did he find such a relic?) standing off to the side as I guess an outbuilding all its own. The totality sprawled more than it ascended. All of its creation was joy.

It's cold out here now—it's almost the end of the year—and though it hasn't snowed yet, it's coming. You can smell it on the listless air. I want to give some word of warning to the boy, tell him he should be dressed warmer, ought to go play someplace safe indoors. But who am I to scold or instruct? I'm out here, too, in my shirt sleeves with two buckets and a rake. How is my activity any different than his? How am I any different from him?

(Need I point out the obvious difference?)

For awhile longer I watch the boy play his construction game. I keep my stupid mouth shut. The wind blows and when it knocks his structure over in a clatter of soda cans and cotter pins and straight-up junk, the boy claps and sings *yay*. I guess falling down's as fun as getting back up. Or maybe I just don't understand how to play. I clap, too, though. Why not? Perhaps some snowflakes begin tumbling on down. The boy starts in again stacking his broken pieces.

THOUGH ONCE again, I've caught myself in a lie. Because I have been back to the university, and not too long ago either. Just a few weeks back, in fact. And I couldn't even tell you why. I had a rare day of feeling both restless and lazy (a dangerous combination), so I forewent the warehouse and bypassed hours of hemming to instead treat myself to a late lunch at the Oral School while the drained November air gathered in the last leaves to the gutters and along the curbs (which—and why do they, curbs?—always look so bereft and forlorn in autumn's thin light), and when I finished my colcannon and finished my Guinness, I buttoned high my slate-grey pilot jacket and walked the few blocks to my former university.

In all these years—and really, how many's it been? six? seven?—since the attack, nearly all the wreckage has been cleared and trucked away, craters backfilled and covered over in grass and wild clover and dandelion gone to seed, most of the blasted and burned buildings demo'd and left as vacant squares while a few like Roman monoliths remained as some bleak reminder as to why things aren't as they were (the charred tower of the carillon I recall loomed like a warning, its scorched bells each distinguishable against the plaster smear of sky), and while at first the campus screamed of abandonment—its quiet interrupted not even by birds—I soon realized this was not entirely so. Some of the remaining residential buildings had been requisitioned for public housing (an empty stroller waited outside the double Napoleon III-style doors of the stone dormitory where I for four years once lived). Counseling and resource centers occupied a handful of academic buildings. And too: art was happening, objects and actions born of grief and reclamation. Though I maybe at first did not recognize what I was seeing.

Because of course, I do not always or even often recognize immediately what things I am seeing. Like the significance of the two most tenuous psyches slow dancing around a wooden swan to Agustín Lara's soulful balladeering. Like Hannah explaining unequivocally that we needed immediately to leave the city while I gazed on in uncomprehending, opiate stupefaction. Now and then as I walked the campus grounds—the empty subbasement sockets of the gone admissions and financial aid offices, the startling unmolestation of the library, the remaining buildings conspicuous as the too-few incisors and cuspids persisting in a set of old gums—I'd find myself approaching dark patches of pavement where obviously some form of ordnance had dropped and gone off: with the superpower of war, the scorches were indelibly worked into the flagstone and cement, a bruise no number of years could wash away. But obviously *not* obvious because I passed so many of these burns before recognizing them for what they were, was in fact walking *through* a swath of blackened concrete before I understood what it was, why it was there, what it meant to have stood in that spot the moment the mark was made. And now in the wake of my empty-headedness, I could see these burns all over. Hundreds of them. And what's more, some were coursing over or really somehow interlaid with a companion burst the same faded grey as old teeth, spreading out in organic tendrils and wisps and sprays, the suggestion of movement reminding me of the way lime builds over the rock formations in caves or the internal stonework of coastal forts. As much as the scorch marks documented the past escape of fire, these ghostly flares seemed to indicate, too, some other, slower kind of reaction, born in the same instant and just as volatile. These discolored markings disturbed me, and were hypnotic.

I had come across at least four or five of these tooth-grey blooms (or anyway, had been aware of four or five) when, in a concrete square enclosed by the university's four identical science buildings, I came upon an Asian woman fast at work with what I took at first to be a refrigerator box. But rather than sturdy cardboard, the box was built of deeply stained wood (not like linseed-oil stained, mind you, but *use* stained, hand and dirt and weather stained). I'd eventually figure out that the box had no top and each panel was hinged on bottom and buckled together on the sides. But at first glance: an Asian woman and a refrigerator box. She also had a steamer trunk.

I guess the only thing now is to breakdown what sequence I witnessed:

- From her steamer trunk, the woman withdrew a corrugated tube—the sort of thing used to mail blueprints or oversized posters or prints—and selected, seemingly at random, four scroll-like charcoal drawings that she then affixed with a gummy putty, one at a time, to each panel of her box.
- The charcoal drawings were abstract and cartoonish in their exaggerated swoops and furls, like billowing friendly ghosts.
- Over each charcoal drawing she applied a clingy sheet of transparency.

- Onto each transparency she began to paint, laying down strokes of what looked like gooey Elmer's craft glue.

- It was around this time I realized the woman and her objects were positioned overtop an enormous black burn seared into the cement.

- The woman had to work fast—despite the paint's viscosity, her thick application dripped and river'd quickly—expertly tracing the arcs and folds of her drawing with swift precision and a two-inch horsehair brush.

- When each side was complete, she'd unbuckle the panel and swing it down on its bottom hinge—sometimes settling it gently and sometimes letting it drop, loudly clapping to the cement—then immediately lift the panel again and buckle it back in place, the transparency now detached from the drawing and plastered to the ground.

- With a measured gesture, she'd peel the transparency off the cement and drape it over the open lid of her trunk.

- On the ground, the transfer of tooth-grey would ooze and pool, at once resembling still the drawings from which the strokes were traced yet also taking on a life and trajectory all their own.

- Paying no attention to the paint crawling across the pavement (beyond what was necessary, of course, to avoid dragging her foot through it), the artist moved on to the next panel in line.

- Sometimes she'd add one liquid or another to thin or thicken the paint.

- When all four panels were complete, she'd rotate the box a one-eighth turn—its bottom edges grinding against the cement beneath—and repeat the process again. New charcoal drawings. New designs in ectoplasmic goo.

I couldn't wait for her to finish. Or I could but didn't want to. Somehow I knew seeing the completed work on its own—without the woman and without her tools, without things happening and instead having happened—would ruin me. I left before the final panel was hinged and pressed to the ground. But between the afternoon's light's decrease and the science buildings' deep shadows flooding the square, it seemed to me that faintly, the pearly designs as they dried glowed mesmerically against the black.

Whether I meant to or not, who can now say, but walking in a daze from the black and grey explosions, I headed toward the hill where Hannah and I had watched the mortars scour across the campus. Maybe I was thinking I'd catch the sunset burning out over the university's remains. Maybe I wasn't thinking at all, my body guiding me of its own accord while my insulated mind folded deeper into itself. Regardless, I emerged from the passage between what I recall once being two freshman dorms, I looked out upon the hillside now rendered in two separate palettes: the lower wash of purples and blues from the shadows already creeping up the slope, and the upper spray of oranges and pinks that always remind me of popsicle melt, brilliant and wistful and capping the hill's crown. And between me and that crown like the scattered graves of a lost cemetery, dozens of low forms projected from the ground. Some broad and squat and some like little towers and others still like dancers captured midpirouette. Though maybe that's a little too fanciful for how the figures *en masse* really looked: an army of dead or undead stubbing up the hill.

I don't know, maybe it was just some seasonal post-Day of the Dead bullshit or the overall context of the memorial campus or maybe it was a pure effect of light, but coming upon this scene unexpectedly, I was just as much thrilled as I was terrified. And more than anything, I was curious.

Which is to say, the sun set before I capped the orange-lit crest. It set before I'd had a chance to visit and inspect even half the figures on the hill. Up close, they were revealed to be constructed of metal frames—maybe aluminum or something else tough that won't visibly oxidize—variously packed and bound with what appeared to be bales of moss and half-rotten straw. But that was just the scaffolding, the canvas and its stretching frame. For out of these bindings exploded amorphous blooms of dense, spongy clouds, plated clusters like ornately painted and compounded gills, trumpets of gold and trumpets of black, buttons of pink, of amethyst, of red.

The sculptures were made of mushrooms.

What's a sunset compared to such an array? I wandered around the hill with my back to the lightshow, completely taken in by each figure I encountered. Some with their bursts of fins and caps looked very much like people or, at the very least, people parts: the roll of a shoulder and topography of a cheek, a brow, a hardy abdominal droop. Others, erupting along the matrix of their frames, resembled the living potential perhaps hidden in the higher functions of Otto's geometries, a kind of mycological fractal. On some, the bales of peat medium had fallen away, freeing the mushrooms to spill from the dropped moss out across the ground. On others, I could tell: new additions had been made. Fresh bindings. Fresh straw.

The last tangerine light had almost rinsed off the hill before I realized I was not alone. Like me, another woman wove among the sculptures, studying each one with (what appeared at that distance, in that light) a dazzled sort of attention. Or maybe it was delight. Our main difference being she was a figure at work, now and then from her rucksack withdrawing a wad of material—more peat? straw? some other rot-eager medium?—and binding it to the frame. More often loading a large syringe and injecting its inoculant into the forms.

Later I would learn that these women—two former classmates of mine, in fact, though I never knew them at the time or (unlikelier) don't remember meeting them—were part of the city's restoration mission to reclaim the landscape from the scars of war, a movement that'd begun even before the fighting had come to an end, each in her own way impressing life and movement to commemorate those forever stilled. But I didn't need to read a city hall brochure to know that. Any idiot could see. Every physical movement and every trace that remained. All of it was loss and all of it was necessary. Portraits of ghosts. Decomposers on a frame. Anyone could see.

I hadn't realized I'd been spotted until she was upon me and already, it was too late. She was smiling and shaved-headed and greeting me with an open hand and what I think might have been a drawled *guten Tag*. She smelled of her cigarettes, and of dark things, and of earth. Her hand was callused and held my hand a little longer than most would generally consider polite, and she asked me something I could not possibly understand. Or maybe it was a reprise of I just didn't want to. Because the delight she radiated was the delight of a mother singing at a funeral, giving voice to the spirit's frequency of grief that's equal to the frequency of amazement that we can ever know anyone at all. It's a song I've maybe had enough of already in this lifetime. I wanted to say the words—to say to her *mycelial sculpture*—but all at once or maybe for a long time without my noticing, I was completely tongue-tied and mute as a stone. So instead I just stared into her deeply lined Germanic face and held the thorn forest of her hand. Is there a word for when you meet a person and simultaneously—immediately—hate them as much as you love them? Or do I mean again something more like being terrified and thrilled? The last light caught her eyes so each iris blazed like amber. Then it went out.

OBSESSED WITH light and obsessed with death and obsessed with the life contained within all death and I guess obsessed, too, with a dilettante's understanding of math and motion and the illusions these things all together create: Where really is a girl to go?

To a room of one's own, of course.

I inhabit the room, and I am the room.

Meanwhile, outside the warehouse it is snowing again, the weather shouldering in against concrete walls, along the framework and glazing of windows. It wants to drift shut the doors. And that's okay. While it's not nearly so warm as it would be on a bright, cloudless day, it's really not so cold inside now. The sky through the glass is a uniform grey, soft and—so it seems— *present*. As in: here with me. And so the light through the windows is muted too. It's worth losing the thermal gain for this company of diffuse light. (To further translate the Vikar's thesis: all light is present in all times, all times present in the light.) The snow falls outside and the dust falls inside, the veils from the ceiling run unmoving to the floor, plate glass kissing glass and cinders kissing rubber, the disseminated light softening even the shadows. The only lines, then, are the ones I've created. Ratios in space, between the inside and out. And even those are growing faint in this pall.

Despite my illusions and my thrall of the light, I know what I've built here isn't art. It's a response. I'm defining the parameters of a vacuum. What is within and what is without. But shining a light on a hole in the wall does not fill the hole, does not fix the wall. I mean, just view it from above:

- A hexagon of fabric.
- A decagon of glass built of triangles of glass.
- A circle of black rubber.
- The passage of light and time.
- I know what I've made isn't art.

Yet it nevertheless reeks of ambition. Maybe I should just stick to my blue postcards to TC, small and simple and easy to disregard (shining a light on one hole without filling the hole). But what about Hannah and Denver? What about Lily and Otto and Marlene? Everyone I cannot reach and everyone who cannot see? How else can I shine a light onto that vacuum? How else can I translate music into form, time into space? Something we together can inhabit.

The muffle of snow. The stillness of what I've made. A chill that has nothing to do with cold. Yet so contained, my heart and my lungs expand and contract. (An excised frame is still only 1/24th a second, emergent from and heading toward every action before or since.) I cannot excise my pulse or my breath. The *whoosh* of blood—I can hear it, it whooshes in my ears, in my veins. If it makes sound, it's moving. If you hear it, you're moving too. The steam-works of my breath distort how I see my fabrication, how the light that is all light describes this time that is all time. But am I the movie or just a frame? The aluminum plate or the phthalo blue? The photograph or the foundry?

These aren't rhetorical questions.

I've elided the planes.

I have brought nearer the walls.

No INSIDENESS and no OUTSIDENESS.

I am contained.

But I am not still.

Everything is never still.

Hurtling through external space while perpetually circulating in the interior. Nothing can stop this violence of motion.

But I cannot deny: it's fun to pretend. Can't deny the allure of living enclosed within a manufactured dream.

ACKNOWLEDGMENTS

THIS BOOK owes its existence to the works and lives of more artists than I can name or even remember. Many—such as Eva Hesse, Robert Irwin, Maya Deren—are cited within the text itself. Others are less overt in how they shaped, informed, and outright inspired not just the backgrounding context of Margaux's world but the images, the events, the very characters of *Enclosure Architect.* Of particular importance is the gestalt of Hanne Darboven, whose body of work (especially *Kulturgeschichte1880–1983*) was the impetus behind and origin of so much of this novel, including the Pigeon Queen's household menagerie, the photograph of a soldier on Otto's mantelpiece, and the entire essence of Marlene. For these people—for their existence and example—I am immeasurably indebted and grateful.

But more so than these variously canonized artworks and artists, it's my lived experiences with so many insatiably curious, creative individuals that have given life to this novel. Particular moments with particular people, so many seconds and minutes and years that cannot possibly be quantified. But since this novel

is partway composed of impossible lists, it is my obligation to at
the very least try.

- Witnessing Dean Thornton—a stranger who, in one year's
  time, would become one of my dearest friends—crouched
  on the filthy floor of a dark, off-campus living room,
  illuminated only by the static glow of a couple flickering TVs
  whose white noise was sometimes audible and sometimes
  not as he contorted his body to shape the feedback swelling
  and subsiding through his guitar and amplifier, building
  with his delay pedals looping echoes of finger-tapped
  melodies while narrating some sort of grief through his
  hoarse voice, through his bob and sway, through his very
  presence: vulnerable and exposed before a room of silhou-
  ette observers.

- Terry James Conrad building an enormous pencil shaped
  like a crutch, then fixing the pencil to the branch of an
  autumn-nude tree in his front yard, a pad of paper beneath
  its sharpened tip so that the tree and the wind could
  together, slowly, draw a picture of their shared experience.

- Armed with a set of dentistry tools and a minidisc recorder:
  JR Sheetz helping me cross the connections of my keyboard's
  circuitry—two mad scientists hunched over a splayed-open
  device in the operating theater of a dormitory basement—
  until the keyboard lost its mind and began performing noisy,
  fractured, beautiful music all on its own while we stood back
  and listened and recorded what we heard.

- Jenna Crowder (we'd only just met) inviting me to create *something* with her in a street-side window space in front of the Maine College of Art. For weeks we improvised movements, symbolically disemboweled one another, bound our heads in cloth, wrote messages in Vaseline and glass, stitched rags into ropes of intestines that we then nailed strand-by-strand to the wall, ate a cow's tongue and sometimes were even kind to one another, all enacted like clockwork on deep-freeze Tuesday nights while friends and strangers and sometimes nobody observed from the sidewalk outside.

- Orondé Cruger calculating the number of ducklings necessary to occupy the volume of my body.

- Gerald Walsh writhing like a gleeful centipede while he described to me in minute detail a Cronenbergian body-horror dream. We hadn't even yet been introduced.

- Helping Alia Ali upholster every single available surface of SPACE Gallery in the most gorgeously patterned textiles over the course of a long May weekend while the rest of the world basked in the sun.

- Derek Kimball attending a local festival of short horror films, deciding that he could make a better short horror film, then proving himself right. Or: Derek introducing me to *Funk & Wagnalls Standard Dictionary of Folklore, Mythology, and Legend.*

- Standing in a mostly empty college venue, bare inches away from Tim Kinsella as he—calm as any shaman or cipher—howled an ancestral hurt that resounds within me to this day.

- The entire semester of Tom Peterson's Myth, Ritual, and the Creative Process.

- Ben Trickey, furious at all the kids dressed up like punks.

- Angela Del Raso, sleeping like a cat in her studio—wheel, elephant ear, buckets of reclaim, jars of *terra sigillata*—waking herself every hour to check the temperature of a gas kiln, night after ceramic night.

- Every X-Acto-knife-and-glue-stick session with Wes Sweetser and Laura Stocklin, snipping apart and reassembling comic books, fashion catalogs, and back issues of *National Geographic* into the most unsettling cartoon collages.

- Convening several nights a week in my kitchen with Justin Woollard, SK Green, and Johnnie Walker, sketching our ids on cheap computer paper for an entire summer and fall.

- Every single concert I ever saw with Noah Morgan, every song we raised our fists to at high velocity on any Western New York highway, every pointless argument about Ohio.

- Zack Wickham destroying the skater kids' apartment or reclined on his midnight porch, picking off frat boys with a BB gun as they stumbled home from our town's one nightclub.

- Hours of free-association with Toccarra Thomas in the swelter of a July night, lounging on her front stoop and drinking pink gin and rosé.

- Andrew Lyman and Michael Dix Thomas alternating who spit on whom while we hammered out our awful punk songs in a basement or a gallery.

- Driving ten hours just to pick up a drum kit, then passing around a guitar with Brandon Schmitt and Eric Schwan in the beery Basement of Fun.

- Sitting at the kitchen table with my brother Jaison back when we were still dumb farm kids in the boonies, he grinning and trance-like pulling narrative threads from the chill air while beside him, I scrawled down the outline to another novel we would never actually compose.

- Susan Morehouse lending me her copies of Denis Johnson's *Jesus' Son* and *Resuscitation of a Hanged Man*. Before encouraging me to stop walking through life headfirst. After smashing her favorite mug to make a point about the necessity of emotional stakes.

- In a crowded restaurant, Mary Stebbins-Taitt looking me dead in the eyes before erupting in the loudest, most unselfconsciously sincere laughter I'd ever heard, giving me permission for the first time in my life to really, truly laugh out loud too. Mary sharing with me her gorgeous and sexually charged poetry in the late August quiet of her cluttered home, every inch of usable space filled with books and manuscripts and art-making tools and, sometimes, a bird preening its lovely green feathers. Mary's mythopoeic romance with Keith. Mary in her radiant selfhood.

- So many high-school nights burnt to embers with Glen Brinkerhoff, driving the vacant and impenetrable darkness of rural back roads or nursing weak truck-stop coffee while

discussing song lyrics, the *Necronomicon*, the girls we
desperately, self-destructively loved.

- Johnny Goodboy belching fire in the Swim House.

- Carmina Escobar kneeling alongside me while we plucked
  the wired guts of a broken piano in the dripping autumn
  woods of I-Park, then declaring with such proud certainty,
  "And the name of our band . . . *is The Touchers*!"

- Elisabeth Pellathy casting my toes in paper.

- Emily Weisgerber casting my arm in plaster.

- Briony Jane Nelly Walsh nested on the opposing couch,
  never once letting me get away with my bullshit.

- Matthew Underwood in his entire ineffability.

- Jacob Cholak fearlessly mapping the twinned absurdity and
  beauty of depression, cinema, and religion (often all at
  once), whether we were racing disastrously across the
  continent, hunkered in a forbidding desert, or playing Xbox
  in my criminally unheated apartment.

- Drinking surprisingly delicious instant coffee with Rob
  Lieber in his illegal attic efficiency when he simultaneously
  put me on the spot and nonchalantly included me in the
  greater community/lineage of artists by asking me: *So how
  does your work contribute to the conversation?*

- Forever my favorite studio mates: Haloumi and Bluedog
  keeping me company on the sunporch, we each in our own
  individual sunbeams while I scattershot composed the
  passages of this novel throughout the best days of 2019. May

your long sleep beneath the garden be peaceful, small friends.

- The nights spent working alongside Megan Grumbling and Nadia Prupis, each assisting the others as we composed our three separate manuscripts that somehow all independently, uniquely hinged on recursion and collaboration and grief.

- Every immersive, warm, alienating, satirical, subversive, austere, elaborate, and/or overwhelming act of live performative literature that I could never have pulled off without the support and assistance of Adam Stockman, Elizabeth Spavento, Scott Sell, Patrick Kiley, Cat Bates, Aleric Vince Nez, Adam Manley, Nat Baldwin, Jason Lesaldo, Bill Roorbach, Mark Priola, Word Portland, NPilar, Lorem Ipsum, Bare Portland, the Bushel Collective, SPACE, and the Maine Writers and Publishers Alliance.

- Meghan Lamb and Randall Brown accepting excerpts to publish in *Bridge* and *Matter Press* (respectively).

- Carl Skoggard and Joseph Holtzman providing space, resources, and the opportunity to finish a fifth and "final" draft while immersed in the Hudson Valley idyll of Camp Nest.

- Everyone at the Hewnoaks Artist Colony, so often providing me a spook-ass setting to make new work.

- Sarah Munroe's keen editorial eye and general exuberance throughout the process of transforming a manuscript into a book.

- And most especially, my creative- and domestic-partner Genevieve Johnson. For all our walks through Mass MOCA, Storm King, DIA Beacon, the Boston Institute of Contemporary Art, the Hirshhorn, the Museo de Arte Moderno, the Luis Barragán House, all the other museums and galleries I'm forgetting or whose names I never knew. For teaching me new ways of experiencing and discussing art. For teaching me new ways of experiencing and discussing the phenomenology of being a person among people. For providing the initial pass/fail rating for most everything I do or think up. For digging in the dirt with me, harvesting food with me, tending to small living things with me. For choosing to continue choosing me each day.

I know there are more of you who helped make this novel possible. But knowing and remembering are so rarely the same thing. I'm grateful for you, nevertheless.

Thank you for reading.

—*Saco, Maine, 2023*